D1384332

The Gourmet Club

The Gourmet Club

A SEXTET

JUN'ICHIRŌ TANIZAKI

TRANSLATED BY
Anthony H. Chambers and Paul McCarthy

KODANSHA INTERNATIONAL
Tokyo • New York • London

ACKNOWLEDGMENT

Anthony Chambers is indebted to Professor Burton Watson's *Records of the Grand Historian* for guiding him through the classical Chinese excerpts that appear in "Manganese Dioxide Dreams." He would also like to thank the Center of Japanese Studies, University of Michigan, in whose 1993 publication *New Leaves: Studies and Translations of Japanese Literature in Honor of Edward Seidensticker* an early version of "The Secret" appeared.

Publication of this work, together with the cost of these translations, was assisted by a grant from the Japan Foundation.

The original titles of these stories, in the order in which they appear in this collection, are "Shōnen" (1911), "Himitsu" (1911), "Futari no chigo" (1918), "Bishoku kurabu" (1919), "Aozuka-shi no hanashi" (1926), and "Kasankamangansui no yume" (1955).

Distributed in the United States by Kodansha America, Inc., 575 Lexington Avenue, New York, N.Y. 10022, and in the United Kingdom and continental Europe by Kodansha Europe Ltd., 95 Aldwych, London WC2B 4JF. Published by Kodansha International Ltd., 17-14 Otowa 1-chome, Bunkyo-ku, Tokyo 112-8652, and Kodansha America, Inc. Copyright © Emiko Kanze 1911, 1918, 1919, 1926, 1955. English translation © Kodansha International 2001. All rights reserved. Printed in Japan.
ISBN 4-7700-2690-0
First edition, 2001
01 02 03 04 05   5 4 3 2 1

CONTENTS

INTRODUCTION

The six stories in this collection are broadly representative of Tanizaki Jun'ichirō's long, varied, and brilliant career. The first two come from 1911, just after the young writer's debut, and their lush style well represents the *tambishugi* or aestheticism with which he was immediately identified—a kind of belated *fin de siècle* manner. The next three stories date from the period between the mid-1910s and mid-1920s when Tanizaki wrote in a somewhat more restrained, realistic manner, and explored themes described by Japanese critics as *ero-guro-nansensu*: the erotic, the grotesque, and the "nonsensical," in the sense of wild or black comedy. ("The Two Acolytes" stands somewhat apart from the other two, more typical stories.) The last piece dates from 1955, by which time Tanizaki was the grand old man of Japanese letters, with ten active years of writing still before him, until his death in 1965. The collection thus spans virtually the whole of the writer's career.

I will not attempt to summarize each story, or subject it to analysis in this short introduction. Instead, I propose to point out certain themes or motifs that run through the collection and indeed through Tanizaki's entire oeuvre.

The story that lends its title to the collection as a whole is "The Gourmet Club." Mishima Yukio once famously said that Tanizaki's fiction was, above all, "delicious," and an international symposium held some years ago in Venice resulted in a volume of papers entitled *A Tanizaki Feast*. The man Tanizaki too was a gourmet, and at times a gourmand. At various times in his life he thoroughly indulged his taste for Western, Chinese, and Japanese cuisines. According to his late wife Matsuko, when young and in his prime he delighted in the rich sauces of French and Chinese food, while in his later years the simpler, more natural flavors of Japanese cooking had more appeal. In "The Gourmet Club" the hero is the president of a dining club whose members are constantly on the lookout for unusual delicacies to stimulate their jaded palates. He discovers a new form of Chinese cuisine in which even the most repellent things can serve as ingredients, and in which the distinction between the foods consumed, the dinnerware, and the hands and fingers of the serving girls becomes, as if by magic, blurred.

Nor is Tanizaki's interest limited only to the receiving end of the alimentary canal. In "Manganese Dioxide Dreams" the diary writer (whose age, occupation, residence, and relations all mirror the real-life Tanizaki, making this one of the more autobiographical of his writings) meditates on the shape and color of his own feces as they lie revealed to his gaze in the water of his Western-style toilet. The French actress Simone Signoret and an unfortunate court lady of ancient China are among the things that float up in the course of the slightly befuddled old man's free associations.

Secrecy is another favorite theme. In "The Secret," the protagonist leads a hidden life in the back streets of downtown Tokyo and disguises his gender under the cosmetics and kimono of a traditional Japanese woman. He becomes involved in a love affair, one of the conditions of which is the secrecy in which the woman concerned envelops herself and her whereabouts; when he penetrates the secret, the charm is lost, and the affair ended. "The Children" centers on what is essentially sado-masochistic play among schoolchildren, the setting for which is a forbidden, exotically Western-style wing of a large mansion—a zone of secrecy. The Chinese dining club in a central district of Tokyo that the Count happens upon in "The Gourmet

Club" is also strictly private, by invitation only, no Japanese allowed; it is only through a peephole in a hidden opium den that he is able to observe the Chinese feast that becomes the inspiration for his own outré banquets. And of course there is "Mr. Bluemound," his name a literal translation of the Japanese "Aozuka," suggesting to the reader an affinity with the "Bluebeard" of legend. Mr. Bluemound too has his secret room, the revelation of whose contents so horrifies the narrator that he eventually sickens and dies. He reveals the secret he has learned to his young wife in a last will and testament discovered and read posthumously, which forms the bulk of the story.

Obsession, usually erotic, is a key theme in many of Tanizaki's works—*The Key* and *Diary of a Mad Old Man* are good examples from the later period. The obsessive desire is typically directed at a woman who is thereby "objectified." This is the core of some feminist critiques of Tanizaki's imaginative world. But one should remember that it *is* imaginative, the free play of fantasy, and not a prescription for living a balanced, healthy life of mature, mutually fulfilling relationships. Tanizaki delights in pushing the obsessional as far as he can, in the direction of horror, or comedy, or both. The menu items that appear toward the end of "The Gourmet Club," Mr. Bluemound's collection of "Real Yurakos," and the elderly diarist's toilet musings in "Manganese Dioxide Dreams" are all examples of that curious mixture of the horrific and the comic. Some readers will no doubt take offense, as did the censors in prewar Japan: portions of "Mr. Bluemound" were excised by government fiat. Tanizaki can hardly have been pleased at having his works cut up by the censors, but he never let it deter him, pursuing his fantasies and obsessions to the limit in his fictional writings.

The one story that is rather untypical of this collection, and is indeed unusual among Tanizaki works, is "The Two Acolytes." Here two boys engaged in religious training on Mt. Hiei are faced with a choice: to remain on the holy mountain or to enter the world outside, with its pleasures and pains—the *ukiyo*, which can mean both "the sad world" or "the floating world," depending on which Chinese characters are used. The former is the more traditional Buddhist interpretation, the latter suggests the world of the pleasure quarters, actors, geisha, courtesans—the world depicted in Saikaku's novels and the woodblock prints of Utamaro. Though from a certain perspective the two readings may come neatly together, with the distinction between the sacred and the profane collapsing, as William R. LaFleur convincingly demonstrates in his writings on Buddhist influences on the traditional literary arts of Japan, in Tanizaki's story the two realms are seen as clearly distinct alternatives. The older boy, from a less distinguished background, chooses to stay in the outside world and indeed claims that its pleasures surpass those of the Buddhist Paradise; the younger boy, whose "good breeding" is several times remarked upon, elects to stay in the monastery and forgo present pleasures for more lasting joys. The lyrical ending of the story has the faithful acolyte attending on the death of a white bird, who loved him vainly in a former life as an Indian woman but will eventually be united with him spiritually in the Pure Land. It is hard to relate this to most of Tanizaki's other writings, but perhaps it is an imaginative working-out, many years later, of a crisis the adolescent Tanizaki underwent. He was very much influenced by a teacher whose interests were philosophic and religious, and at one time planned to pursue those paths. In time, though, he came to realize that his own destiny was tied to the world of beauty, both as the object of sensuous desire and the subject of aesthetic endeavor. In terms of the story, he made the choice of the older of the two acolytes, leaving the holy mountain for "the floating world" outside. In this story, he seems to pay tribute to the part of himself that might have chosen the other path.

A few remarks about Japanological matters seem in order. The ages of Tanizaki's characters are given in the traditional *kazoedoshi* count, which means that they are one or two years older than they would be by Western count. The reader should mentally subtract one or two years (it is impossible to say which without knowing birth dates) from their ages as given in the text to arrive at a Western approximation. Except on the jacket, title page, and copyright page of this volume, Japanese names appear in the Japanese order, surnames preceding personal names. The names of Buddhist deities are given in their Japanese form in "The Two Acolytes": thus, Kannon rather than Avalokiteśvara, Monju rather than Manjuśri, etc., since these are the forms that would seem natural to the characters themselves. On the other hand, in "The Secret," where Buddhist references are intended to exoticize the protagonist's surroundings, and he himself has no interest in them as objects of religious devotion, they have been rendered in more recondite Sanskrit form.

Finally, on a personal note, Anthony Chambers and I have been planning some sort of Tanizaki collaboration for many years; this collection of translated stories is the fruit of those plans. The editorial work of Stephen Shaw and Moriyasu Machiko of Kodansha International has been invaluable, and we gratefully acknowledge it. We would both like to dedicate this volume to Howard S. Hibbett and Edward G. Seidensticker, illustrious translators of Tanizaki and our mutual mentors and friends.

Paul McCarthy
February 2001
Tokyo

The Children

TRANSLATED BY
Anthony H. Chambers

Some twenty years have passed since then. It was when I'd finally reached the age of ten and was attending Arima Primary School, behind Suitengū Shrine, from our home in the second block of Kakigara-chō. The sky over Ningyō-chō Avenue was hazy and the sun shone warmly on the dark blue shop curtains, in that genial season when even my idle, dreamy young mind could sense the spring.

One mild, clear day, after our drowsy afternoon classes had ended, I was about to leave the school grounds, gripping an abacus in my ink-stained hands, when someone called my name—"Hagiwara Ei-chan!"—and pattered up behind me. It was my classmate Hanawa Shin'ichi, widely known as a mollycoddle who had never been seen without a housemaid at his side, from the time we began primary school until now, our fourth year: a pampered boy who had no playmates, because everyone had heard that he was a weakling and a crybaby.

"Yes?" It was unusual for Shin'ichi to call out to me. Puzzled, I peered at the maid's face.

"Won't you come play at my house today? We're celebrating the Inari festival in the garden." From lips as red as a strip of scarlet cord, Shin'ichi spoke in a small, timid voice and with a pleading look. Why would this child who always cowered in a corner by himself come out with this unexpected suggestion? Flustered, I tried to read his face. He was always being teased for being a sissy, but now, up close, I could see that he had a certain nobility to his looks, as one might

"Here, young man, try some sweet saké, you needn't pay for it."
As I came to a sweet-saké stand, a smiling maidservant, her long
sleeves tied up with a red cord, called out to me, but I passed with a
scowl. When I arrived before an *oden* stand, I was hailed by an old,
bald fellow. "Here—have some *oden*, it's free, you know."

"I don't want any, I don't want any," I said despondently. Ready to
give up, I headed for the back gate, when a man in a dark blue
happi coat and smelling of saké appeared from nowhere.

"You haven't had any cakes yet, have you, sonny?" he said in thick
Tokyo dialect. "If you're leaving, take some cakes with you. Here,
hand this to the woman at the house over there, and she'll give you
some. Hurry up, now." He handed me a bright red ticket. Self-pity
welled up in my breast, but then I thought that I might be able to see
Shin'ichi if I went to the house, so I took the ticket and started back
through the garden.

Happily, Shin'ichi's housemaid found me in no time.

"Thank you for coming, we've been expecting you. Let's go over
there, away from all those nasty children." As she gently took my
hand, my eyes filled with tears and I couldn't reply right away.

Skirting a veranda whose floor was almost my own height, and
going around behind a spacious wing that projected into the garden,
we arrived in front of a small set of rooms shut off by a bush-clover
fence in a courtyard of about forty square yards.

"Master Shin'ichi, your friend is here," the maid called out, and
from the shade of a clump of Chinese parasol trees, a patter of quick
little steps could be heard from behind the *shōji*.

"Come up here," Shin'ichi yelled as he ran out onto the veranda.
What button had this child pressed to produce such a cheerful voice,
I wondered. My friend was so richly dressed that he looked like a
different person. I gazed up at him, dazzled. As he stood there in a
black *habutae*-silk ceremonial robe adorned with family crests and

topped off with a formal half-coat and divided skirt, the twilled black silk of his half-coat, bathed in the bright sun that illuminated the veranda, glittered like silver dust.

Taking my hand, Shin'ichi led me to a neat little room of eight mats. A sweetness like the fragrance that lingers in the bottom of a cake-box filled the room, and two plump cushions of glossy *hattan* silk had been placed there invitingly. Tea and cakes were brought in immediately, and steamed rice with red beans and delectable side dishes in high-footed lacquer bowls.

"Master Shin'ichi, your mother wants you to enjoy these with your friend. . . . And since you're wearing nice clothes today, please play quietly and don't misbehave." As I was holding back shyly, the maid urged me to try the rice with red beans and some mashed sweet potatoes with sweetened chestnuts. Then she withdrew to an ante-chamber.

It was a quiet, sunny room. A red plum tree by the veranda cast its shadow on the *shōji* paper, which blazed in the sunlight. From the garden in the distance came the *ten-ten-ten* of festival drums, mingled with the excited voices of children. I felt as though I'd come to a strange, faraway country.

"Shin-chan, do you always use this room?"

"No, this is my big sister's place. She has lots of fun toys. Shall I show you?" From a floor-level cupboard Shin'ichi pulled out a Nara doll in the shape of a figure from the Noh play *Shōjō*, wooden dolls dressed in fabric representing the old man and woman in *Takasago*, miniature dolls from Kyoto, Fushimi dolls, and Izukura dolls; and after arranging them neatly around us, he brought out a lot of clay heads of men and women, each attached to a bamboo stick which he thrust into the cracks between the floor mats. Lying on the cushions, we peered at the cleverly made dolls with their beards and protruding eyes, and imagined a world inhabited by these tiny people.

"There are lots of picture books here, too," said Shin'ichi. From another cupboard he dragged a folding-paper case decorated with portraits of the kabuki actors Hanshirō and Kikunojō and stuffed with illustrated storybooks, an assortment of which he showed me. Though a good many years old, the rich woodblock-print coloring of the Mino paper cover glowed brightly, having lost none of its luster. He opened it to reveal pictures of beautiful men and women in the age of the shoguns. From their vivid faces to the tips of their fingers and toes, they seemed to be alive, moving about on the surface of the fuzzy, moldy-smelling paper. In a palace courtyard not unlike the one we were in, a princess was chasing fireflies with her ladies-in-waiting; at the lonely foot of a bridge, a samurai in a deep wicker hat had beheaded a menial and was reading by moonlight the letter he'd taken from a letter case seized from the folds of the corpse's kimono. In the next one, a masked villain dressed in black had stolen into a palace room and thrust his sword through a cushion, into the throat of a sleeping woman whose hair was done in the fashion of a palace attendant. In another, a bewitching woman stood in her nightdress in a room dimly lit by a paper-covered lamp; holding in her mouth a razor dripping with blood, she glared at the corpse of a man lying at her feet, his hands clutching at air, and said derisively, "Look at you now." The illustrations that both Shin'ichi and I enjoyed most were outrageous scenes of murder—victims with their eyes popping out, people cut in half and standing only from the waist down, strange pictures speckled with black, cloud-like bloodstains—and we lost ourselves in gazing at them.

"Shin-chan! There you are, misbehaving again, with things that don't belong to you!" A girl of thirteen or fourteen, dressed in a long-sleeved kimono of Yūzen silk, slid open the door and came rushing in. Brows knit, eyes and mouth imperious, her face was full of child-ish anger as she stood there looking daggers at her little brother and me. I expected Shin'ichi to cringe and turn pale, but he surprised me.

"Nonsense. I'm not misbehaving, I'm just showing these to my friend." Utterly unconcerned, he went on browsing in the picture book without even looking at her.

"But I told you not to play with them!" She pattered up to us and tried to snatch away the book we were looking at, but Shin'ichi wouldn't let go. The cover and the pages were being pulled in two directions, and the binding seemed about to give way as the two glared at each other.

"Stingy!" cried Shin'ichi finally. "Who wants to borrow them anyway?" He flung the book at her, and then threw all the Nara dolls within reach at his sister's face. Missing the mark, they struck the wall of the alcove.

"There, you see how naughty you are—you've hit me again, haven't you? All right, hit me all you want. Thanks to you, I've still got this bruise from the last time. I'm going to show Father and tell him all about it, just you remember." With tears of reproach, she hiked up the skirt of her crepe kimono and showed us a bruise imprinted on her pure white leg. The veins showed blue through the thin, soft skin, and a painful-looking purple blotch stained her leg from the knee to the calf.

"Go ahead and tell. Stingy!" Scattering the dolls with his foot, Shin'ichi then said to me, "Let's go play in the garden," and ran from the room with me in tow.

"But she's crying, isn't she?" I said when we got outside, feeling sorry for his sister.

"Let her cry. It happens all the time—we're always fighting. She may be my sister, but she's not my mother's daughter."

With this brash outburst, Shin'ichi walked toward the shade of some large zelkovas and hackberries, between the Japanese and Western-style houses. The luxuriant branches of the ancient trees screened the sunlight there, allowing green moss to cover the moist ground. A dark, chill current of air seemed to blow down the backs of our necks. There was a body of water, neither a bog nor a pond but most likely the remains of a well, and in it water plants floated like verdigris. Sitting at the edge of the water, the two of us lazily stretched our legs as we inhaled the scent of the damp soil, when the sounds of a subtle, mysterious music reached us.

"What's that?" I asked, listening closely.

"That's my sister playing the piano."

"What's a piano?"

"She says it's like an organ. A foreign woman comes every day to teach her in the Western-style house." Shin'ichi pointed to the second floor. The strange sounds floated out from a window draped with pink fabric . . . now like the echo of a goblin's laughter deep in the woods, now like the dance of fairy-tale dwarves . . . weaving odd fantasies from thousands of colorful threads of imagination in my young head. It was as if they rose up from the depths of the little marsh.

When the music ended, the trance I was in lingered on as I stared at the second floor, longing for the face of a foreigner or of the sister to appear at the window.

"Shin-chan, don't *you* play up there?"

"Mother says I mustn't be bad and go in there. I tried to sneak in once, but it was locked and I couldn't get it open." Shin'ichi, too, looked up at the second floor with eyes full of curiosity.

Just then, someone came running up behind us, asking if he could play with us. He was a pupil at the Arima School, one or two years above us. I didn't know his name, but I knew his face well because he was a notorious bully who was always tormenting the younger children. What's he doing here, I wondered, and watched in silence. Though Shin'ichi called him simply "Senkichi," the other boy fawned on him, addressing him as "the young master." When I asked later, I learned that he was the son of the Hanawas' groom, but at the time the way Shin'ichi treated him seemed like a circus belle taming a wild animal.

"Then we'll play cops and robbers. Ei-chan and I will be the policemen, and you can be the robber."

"Okay, but no rough stuff like the last time. You always tie me up with a rope and wipe your snot on me or something."

This exchange was even more astonishing to me. Try as I might, I simply couldn't picture the sweet, girlish Shin'ichi tying up that rowdy, bearlike Senkichi and torturing him.

Before long, Shin-chan and I were policemen weaving our way around the marsh and through the groves in pursuit of the robber Senkichi; but he was older than we were and, even though we out-numbered him, he was hard to catch. Finally we tracked him to a storehouse in a corner of the wall behind the Western-style house.

Exchanging secret signals, we held our breath and tiptoed into the storehouse. Senkichi was nowhere to be seen. The stifling, musty smell of rice-bran pickle paste and soy-sauce kegs, with sowbugs crawling among the cobwebs on the ceiling and around the kegs, all seemed designed to incite us children to delicious mischief. Then we heard a muffled giggle; a wicker trunk suspended from a beam creaked. "Boo!" cried Senkichi, showing his face from the trunk.

"Come down, right now, or you'll be sorry," shouted Shin'ichi. He and I tried to poke at Senkichi's face with a broom.

"Come and get me. If anyone gets close, I'll pee on him."

Senkichi was about to carry out his threat when Shin'ichi went under the trunk, picked up a bamboo pole, and began to poke wildly at Senkichi's buttocks and thighs through gaps in the wicker.

"Now will you come down?"

"Ow, ow! Okay—sorry—I'm coming!" Senkichi descended meekly, rubbing his injuries.

Seizing the culprit by the lapels, Shin'ichi began a wild interrogation. "What've you stolen, and where? Confess!" Senkichi's response was equally wild, and villainous as well. He'd taken five bolts of fabric from Shirokiya, stolen dried bonito from Nimben's, and pocketed some bills at the Bank of Japan.

"You crook, you've done other bad things, too, haven't you? Did you ever kill anyone?"

"Yes, I did. I killed a masseur on the Kumagaya embankment and stole his purse, containing fifty gold pieces. I spent the money on women in Yoshiwara." It was a quick-witted reply, drawn presumably from something he'd heard at a cheap theater or in a peep show.

"I'll bet you've killed others, besides that. Ah! You won't tell us? If you don't speak up, we'll use torture."

"That's all there is to tell." Senkichi clasped his hands together, begging forgiveness, but Shin'ichi paid no attention. Loosening Senkichi's soiled, pale yellow muslin sash, he used it to bind the boy's hands behind him, and with the remainder deftly tied his ankles. Slyly moving his fingertips, as delicate and pale as those of a child actor or a young geisha, he pulled Senkichi's hair; pinched his cheeks; turned up his eyelids to expose the pink underside and bare the white of his eyes; and grasped his earlobes and the sides of his mouth and shook them. The muscles of Senkichi's coarse, unattractively chubby face stretched and contracted comically like rubber.

When he tired of this, Shin'ichi said, "Wait, wait. You're a criminal, so we'll tattoo your forehead." Pulling a lump of charcoal from a coal sack, he spat on it and began rubbing it on Senkichi's brow. Senkichi, his face now smeared all over with the stuff, twisted his features grotesquely and wailed, but finally seemed to flag and just let his adversary do as he would. The sight of this burly, rough, schoolyard bully reduced by Shin'ichi to such a state, making faces like some kind of hobgoblin, gave me a strange sense of pleasure I'd never experienced before; but fearful of the retribution that would come at school tomorrow, I felt no wish to join in Shin'ichi's mischief.

When he was finally untied, Senkichi glared resentfully at Shin'ichi, then crumpled to the floor, where he lay face down, motionless and silent. When we tried to pull him up by the arms, he slumped back again. Worried, the two of us quietly stood watching him.

"Hey, is something wrong?" Shin'ichi grabbed his collar roughly and turned his face up. Pretending to cry, Senkichi had rubbed half the muck off his face with his narrow sleeves. The effect was so comical that all three of us burst out laughing.

"Let's play something else."

"No more rough stuff, please, Master Shin'ichi. Look at these marks." The sash had left red abrasions on Senkichi's wrists where he'd been tied up.

"I'll be a wolf, and you two be travelers, okay? At the end you'll both be eaten up by the wolf."

I felt uneasy when Shin'ichi said this, but Senkichi replied, "Let's do it!" and I had to go along. Senkichi and I were travelers stopping for the night in this storage shed, which was now a roadside temple. Shin'ichi the wolf attacked in the middle of the night, howling outside the door. Finally the wolf chewed through the door and entered on all fours, emitting an outlandish growl which sounded like a cross between a dog and a cow. Shin'ichi took his role very seriously as he chased the fleeing travelers, and I began to worry about what might happen to me when I was caught. With an anxious smile, I scrambled frantically across the straw bags and behind the kegs in an effort to escape.

"Hey, Senkichi," cried the wolf. "Your leg's been bitten and you can't walk any more." The wolf had trapped one of the travelers in a corner of the temple. When the wolf pounced and began biting him all over his body, Senkichi grimaced and gaped like an actor in a skillful display of agony. Finally, his windpipe severed by the wolf's teeth, he screamed, his arms and legs shook, and, clutching at air, he collapsed.

Now it was my turn. Terrified, I jumped up on top of a keg, but the wolf caught the hem of my kimono in his mouth and pulled with appalling strength. Deathly pale, I clutched the keg, but when I saw the wolf's ferocious look, I lost heart. *There's no escape*, I told myself. No sooner had I shut my eyes in resignation than I was dragged down to the earthen floor, where I lay on my back. Quick as a gust of wind, Shin'ichi was at my throat and severed my windpipe.

"You're both dead now, so you can't move, no matter what. I'm going to suck the marrow from every bone in your bodies."

Following Shin'ichi's instructions, the two of us lay motionless, sprawling where we'd fallen on the floor, our arms and legs out-stretched. A cold draft blew through an opening in my kimono and against my crotch, and the tip of the middle finger of my outflung right hand could just feel Senkichi's hair.

"This plump one looks tasty, I'll eat him up first." Shin'ichi looked pleased as he crawled on top of Senkichi's body.

Senkichi opened his eyes a crack. "Don't overdo it," he pleaded in a whisper.

"I won't, just don't move." Smacking his lips greedily, he nibbled at the head and face, chest and belly, both arms, and from the thighs to the shins, in the process treading on the eyes, nose, and breast with his dirty sandals, so that Senkichi was again covered with muddy marks.

"Now for the hip meat!" Senkichi was turned over so that he lay face down, and his kimono was hitched up abruptly, exposing his naked body from the waist down, like a pair of scallions lined up side by side. Folding the skirt of the kimono over the corpse's head and jumping onto his back, Shin'ichi made a great show of smacking his lips again. Senkichi endured everything patiently. The exposed skin was all gooseflesh, apparently from the chilly air, and his but-tocks quivered like jelly.

I knew I was soon going to find myself in the same position, and my heart pounded secretly at the thought, but I didn't expect to be treated as badly as Senkichi had been. Eventually Shin'ichi straddled my chest and began to eat the tip of my nose. In my ears I heard the rustle of the lining of his Kai silk half-coat; my nose picked up the fragrance of camphor incense in his kimono; my cheeks were brushed by the soft *habutae* fabric; my chest and belly felt the weight of his warm body. The strange sensation of his moist lips and the smooth tip of his tongue as he tickled and licked erased my fears and won me over, as though I'd been bewitched, until at last I began to feel pleasure. Suddenly my face was being trampled on, from the hair on the left side to the right cheek, and my nose and lips were rubbed in the mud on the soles of his sandals; but this, too, was pleasurable, and before I knew it I was enjoying being turned, body and soul, into Shin'ichi's puppet.

Finally I was rolled over onto my face, my kimono was hiked up, and I was devoured from the waist down. Shin'ichi laughed with delight at the sight of two corpses lined up on the earthen floor, our buttocks exposed. But just then the housemaid appeared at the door of the storehouse. Senkichi and I leapt to our feet in surprise.

"Master Shin'ichi! Is this where you've been? Look at the mess you've made of your clothes. Why do you have to play in such filthy places? *You're* to blame, Sen-chan." As she scolded us, the housemaid looked at Senkichi's face, which was still smeared with muddy footprints. I stood there petrified, my trampled face smarting, feeling the way one does after committing some dire offense.

"That's enough of your playing—go on up to the house and take a hot bath, it's ready now, or your mother will be furious. Master Hagiwara, I hope you'll come again. It's late; shall I take you home?" She was gentle with me.

"You don't need to, I can go alone," I said, excusing myself. The three of them saw me to the gate. "Bye," I said.

Outside, I found that a blue evening haze had settled over the streets, and lamps were flickering on the road along the river. Feeling as though I'd returned abruptly to the city after a disturbing visit to some foreign place, I headed home, recalling the day's events as though they were a dream. Shin'ichi's aristocratic looks and his high-handed way of treating people stayed on my mind for the rest of the day.

When I arrived at school the next morning, Senkichi, the object of such torment yesterday, was lording it as always over a large group of weaklings, while Shin'ichi was his usual mollycoddle self, shrink-ing away in a corner of the playground with his maid.

"Shin-chan, do you want to play?" I called.

"No." He scowled and shook his head crossly.

Four or five days later, Shin'ichi's maid accosted me again after school. "Today his sister's dolls are set up for the Doll Festival," she said. "Won't you come and play again?"

This time I entered the grounds through the front gate, with a bow to the porter, and opened the lattice door next to the main entrance to the house. Senkichi came bounding out immediately and led me through the corridors to a ten-mat room on the mezzanine. Shin'ichi and his elder sister, Mitsuko, lay sprawled before a tiered doll stand, eating roasted beans; but the moment the two of us came in they began to giggle, as though they were hatching some outrageous mis-chief again.

"What's funny, Master Shin'ichi?" Senkichi said uneasily, peering at their faces.

The tiers of the doll stand were covered with a red woolen cloth. High above it all were the roof tiles of a palace building that looked like the Kannon temple in Asakusa. Lined up inside the hall were the emperor and empress, court musicians, and court ladies; below the

Cherry Tree of the Left Guards and the Orange Tree of the Right Guards, three groundsmen were warming some saké. The next tier was decorated with candlestands, trays, implements for blackening the teeth, and dainty little furnishings with arabesque designs in gold lacquer, together with the various dolls that had been in Mitsuko's room several days before.

As I stood, captivated, before the doll stand, Shin'ichi crept up behind me and whispered, "We're going to get Senkichi drunk on white saké." Moving over to Senkichi, he said nonchalantly, "Hey, let's the four of us have a drinking party."

Sitting in a circle, we began to drink white saké, with roasted beans on the side.

"This saké is absolutely first-class," said Senkichi, making us laugh with his imitation of an adult's way of talking, as he gulped the stuff down from a tea cup held in the same way as a saké cup. Expecting him to get drunk at any moment, Mitsuko clutched her sides, barely able to contain the mirth that welled up inside her; but by the time Senkichi was getting tipsy, his three companions had reached a similar state as well. The warm saké simmered and seethed in my belly, sweat broke out on my forehead and temples; the crown of my head felt oddly numb, and the surface of the floor mats swayed up and down, left and right, like the bottom of a ship.

"I'm drunk, Master Shin'ichi. All of you are red in the face, too. Let's stand up and see if we can walk!" Senkichi rose and took a step, swinging his arms triumphantly, but immediately staggered and fell, bumping his head against the alcove post and making the rest of us burst out laughing.

"Ow! Ow!" he said, rubbing his head and frowning; but then he gave a snort himself, overcome with merriment.

Following Senkichi's example, the rest of us stood up, tried to walk, and fell over; falling over, we laughed; and soon we were raising a terrible ruckus, shrieking and feeling very pleased with ourselves.

"Ah, that feels good! I'm drunk, dammit!" Tucking up the skirt of his kimono, Senkichi strutted around like a craftsman, with his arms inside his kimono and fists on his shoulders. Shin'ichi and I, and finally even Mitsuko, tucked our skirts into our sashes, thrust our fists up to our shoulders just like Miss Kichiza in the kabuki play, and marched unsteadily around the room, crying "Dammit, I'm drunk!" and rolling over with laughter.

"Hey, Master Shin'ichi! Shall we play Fox?" said Senkichi, as if he'd had a brilliant idea. The plan was that Senkichi and I would be two peasants out to get rid of a fox, but instead we'd be bewitched by Mitsuko—a fox in the form of a woman—and then rescued by Shin'ichi, a passing samurai, who would dispose of the animal himself.

Still drunk, the three of us agreed immediately and began our drama. First, Senkichi and I made our entrance. Wearing twisted towels around our heads and brandishing dusters, we said, "Seems like a wicked fox has been up to no good in these parts. Let's have a go at getting rid of him today."

Mitsuko the fox came toward us from the other side, saying, "Hello, hello. Come on—follow me, and I'll give you something good to eat." She tapped us on the shoulder, and instantly we fell under her spell.

"Well, well! Ain't she a lovely lady!" we said, making eyes at her.

Mitsuko seemed to be having a wonderful time. "You're bewitched now, both of you, so if I give you a turd to eat, you've got to gulp it down." Giggling, she heaped up filthy piles of bean-jam dumplings she'd already bitten into, buckwheat buns she'd crushed underfoot, and roasted beans she'd kneaded with snot. Then, after setting the plates out before us, she spat phlegm and saliva into some white saké and said, "Pretend this isn't saké but pee. Here, gentlemen, have a drink!"

"Oh, it's delicious, delicious," we cried, devouring everything hungrily, though the white saké and beans tasted strangely salty.

"Now I'll play the shamisen for you. You have to dance with plates on your heads." Using a duster as her shamisen, Mitsuko began to sing, "*Korya, korya.*" Senkichi and I placed cake plates on our heads and danced in rhythm, crying "*Yoi kita, yoi ya sa.*"

When Shin'ichi the samurai happened upon us, he saw right through the fox's disguise. "You're a scoundrel, bewitching humans like this when you're just an animal. I'm going to tie you up and kill you, so prepare yourself!"

"Shin-chan, if you get rough I won't play any more."

Hating to come in second in anything, the spirited Mitsuko grappled with Shin'ichi, revealing her true, tomboy character as she stubbornly refused to submit.

"Senkichi, lend me your sash so I can tie up this fox. Then the two of you hold down her feet so she can't struggle."

One of the picturebook illustrations I'd seen, which depicted a young samurai joining forces with a lackey to rob a beautiful woman, came to mind as I helped Senkichi pin her in place by grasping her firmly through the skirts of her Yūzen kimono and holding her legs. While we did this, Shin'ichi, with some difficulty, tied Mitsuko's hands behind her back and then lashed her to the veranda railing.

"Ei-chan, take off her sash and use it to gag her."

"Right!" I promptly moved behind Mitsuko, undid her saffron crepe waistband, and, taking care not to disturb her freshly done Tōjin coiffure, insinuated my hands around the back of her neck. I wrapped the band twice beneath her chignon—moist with oil—grazing her ears and covering her chin, then pulled as hard as I could, so that the crepe dug into the flesh of her plump cheeks. Mitsuko made writhing motions, like the Snow Princess in the puppet play *The Temple of the Golden Pavilion.*

"Now you get your own shit torture."

Grabbing some soft rice cakes, Shin'ichi stuffed them in his mouth, then began spitting pieces at Mitsuko's face. As we looked on delightedly, the Snow Princess's beautiful complexion turned into something repulsive, like the face of a leper or a syphilitic.

Senkichi and I were hooked. "You filthy animal, you had a lot of nerve, making us eat that dirty stuff, didn't you?" We joined Shin'ichi in spitting at her until, deciding that this treatment was too lenient, we soiled every inch of Mitsuko's face, rubbing bits of rice cake and crushing bean-jam cakes against her forehead and cheeks, then daubing her with the crusts of Daifuku cakes. She looked like a featureless monster, eyes and nose indistinguishable in a dark smear— an ogre wearing a Tōjin hairdo and an enchanting, long-sleeved kimono, for the moment like some creature from a ghost story. Mitsuko seemed to have lost the will to resist: she lay there obediently as if dead, no matter what we did to her.

"I'll let you off with your life, just this time. If you ever bewitch a human again, I'll kill you." The moment Shin'ichi loosened her gag and untied her bonds, Mitsuko jumped up, went out through the sliding door, and fled, pattering down the corridor.

"Master Shin'ichi, she's angry and she's gone to tell on us." Senkichi exchanged anxious glances with me, as if finally aware that we'd done something inexcusable.

"Who cares if she tells?" Shin'ichi said with arrogant indifference. "She's too pleased with herself, so I pick fights and tease her all the time." As he spoke, the door slid open quietly and Mitsuko, her face washed clean, came back. She had washed off her white makeup along with the bean jam, so that she looked fresher and brighter than before, and her beautiful bare skin was all the more lustrous. I waited for her to start another quarrel, but instead she was quite straightforward about it all.

"It would've been embarrassing if anyone had seen me, so I slipped into the bath and washed it off. . . . You're all so rough." She smiled brightly.

Emboldened by this, Shin'ichi announced, "This time I'll be a human, and the three of you can be dogs. I'll toss cakes and stuff to you, and you'll get down on all fours and eat them. Okay?"

Senkichi dropped down on his hands and knees and, saying "Right, I'm a dog now, woof, woof," trotted cheerfully around the room. As I followed along, right on his tail, something moved Mitsuko to say, "I'm a female dog." Joining us, she crawled around the room.

"Here, sit up, sit up. . . . Wait for the command before you eat." After we'd been put through our paces, Shin'ichi cried "Start!" and we dashed for the cakes, each of us trying to be first.

"I have a good idea. Wait, wait." Shin'ichi left the room but soon came back with two real Japanese spaniels, clad in sleeveless jackets, and turned them loose among us. With half-eaten jam cakes and buns smeared with snot and saliva now scattered all over the floor mats, the three "dogs" and two spaniels scrambled to reach the prizes and piled on top of one another, baring their teeth, sticking out their tongues, biting into the same cakes, and licking each other's noses.

When they'd eaten up the cakes, the spaniels began to lick Shin'-ichi's fingertips and the soles of his feet. Not to be outdone, the three of us followed suit.

"It tickles, it tickles." Leaning against the veranda railing, Shin'ichi held out his soft, white soles toward each of our noses in turn.

People's feet taste salty and sour. On a nice-looking person, even the toenails look nice. With such thoughts in mind, I sucked at the spaces between his toes.

Growing more and more excited, the spaniels lay on their backs pawing the air, and tugged at the hem of his kimono with their teeth. Delighted, Shin'ichi stroked their faces with his feet and rubbed their bellies. When I imitated them and tugged at his hem, the soles of Shin'ichi's feet touched my cheeks and stroked my forehead, just as he'd done with the spaniels, but when he pressed a heel against my eye or covered my mouth with the arch of his foot it wasn't as much fun.

We played this way until evening, when I went home. From the next day on I visited the Hanawa home almost daily and could hardly wait for my classes to end. Day and night, images of Shin'ichi and Mitsuko never left my mind. Shin'ichi's willfulness got worse and worse as I gradually grew accustomed to it, until I'd become as completely his follower as Senkichi was; and whenever we played I was pummeled or tied up. Strangely, even his headstrong sister was utterly submissive after the eradication of the fox: she never defied Shin'ichi, nor indeed even me or Senkichi, and at times she herself would suggest "Shall we play Fox?" It began to look as though she enjoyed being bullied.

Every Sunday Shin'ichi would go to a toy shop in Asakusa or Ningyō-chō. When he came back with armor and swords, he'd immediately begin to wave them around, so that Mitsuko, Senkichi, and I were never without bruises somewhere on our bodies. As time went by and we began to run out of games, we'd devise various other plans, using the storehouse, the bath, or the inner garden as stages on which to give ourselves over to violent play. Whenever Senkichi and I strangled Mitsuko and stole her money, Shin'ichi would avenge his sister by killing the two of us and taking our heads. Or Shin'ichi and I—two villains—would poison the young lady and her faithful retainer Senkichi and throw their bodies into the river. The worst roles and harshest treatment always fell to Mitsuko. Finally we resorted to putting rouge and paint on our bodies, so that when one of us was killed we'd be covered with blood as we rolled around in agony. It reached the point where Shin'ichi would sometimes produce a real knife and say, "Let me cut you just a little with this, okay? Only a little bit—it won't hurt that much." Then the three of us would meekly allow ourselves to be pinned underfoot.

"Don't cut too much," we'd say, waiting stoically as if we were about to undergo surgery, and yet we'd look on fearfully with tears in our eyes as we let him cut our shoulders and knees and watch the blood flow from our wounds. When I returned home each evening and took a bath with my mother, I went to great pains to hide the marks from her.

These games continued for about a month. Then, one day, when I went as usual to the Hanawa house I found Senkichi there all by himself with nothing to do, as Shin'ichi had gone to the dentist.

"What about Mit-chan?"

"She's having her piano lesson. Shall we go over to the Western house? That's where she is." Senkichi led me to the little marsh in the shade of those huge trees. Immediately caught up in the music, I sat at the base of an ancient zelkova and listened to the sounds that flowed from the second-floor window. The first day I'd visited this estate, I'd sat with Shin'ichi at the edge of the same marsh and listened with him to this same strange music—now like the echo of a goblin's laughter deep in the woods, now like the dance of fairy-tale dwarves, weaving odd fantasies from thousands of colorful threads of imagination in my young head—and today again, just as then, we could hear it coming from the second-floor window.

When the performance ended, I turned to Senkichi with the same curiosity I'd felt before. "Sen-chan, haven't you ever gone up there, either?"

"Hardly anyone goes there except Miss Mitsuko and Tora-san, who does the cleaning. It's not just me, her brother doesn't know what's up there, either."

"I wonder what it's like inside."

"I hear there're lots of funny newfangled things their father bought overseas. Once I asked Tora-san to let me take a peek, but he wouldn't hear of it. . . . The lesson's over. Shall we call her, Ei-chan?"

Together we shouted toward the second floor.

"Mit-chan, let's play!"

"Miss Mitsuko, won't you play with us?"

There was only silence. It was enough to make me wonder if the music we'd been listening to might not have been the faint reverberation produced spontaneously by the piano in a deserted room.

"I guess just the two of us will have to play, then." With only Senkichi as a companion, we wouldn't have as much fun as usual. Losing interest, I stood up, when suddenly I heard a snort of laughter behind us. There stood Mitsuko.

"We were just calling you, why didn't you answer?" Turning toward her, I looked at her reproachfully.

"Where did you call me?"

"From below the window, when you were practicing in the Western house. Couldn't you hear us?"

"I haven't been in the Western house. No one can go in there."

"But you were just playing the piano, weren't you?"

"Not me. Must have been someone else."

Senkichi had been following this exchange suspiciously. "We know you're lying. How about it?—how about taking Ei-chan and me up there on the sly? Or do you insist on telling fibs? If you don't come clean, this is what you'll get." With a ghastly smirk, he grabbed Mitsuko's wrist and began to twist, slowly and firmly.

"Oh, Senkichi, don't—please! I'm not lying, I promise you!" Though she assumed a pleading expression, she neither raised her voice nor tried to run away, but simply squirmed as her arm was twisted. I found the contrast between the two children's complexions—the pale skin of her fragile limb, gripped by his steely fingers—curiously appealing.

"Mit-chan," I said, "we'll torture you if you don't confess." Twisting her other arm, I undid her waistband and tied her to the trunk of an oak tree near the marsh. "Do you give up? Not yet?" As usual the two of us applied ourselves to punishing her with pinches and tickles.

"When your brother gets home, you'll have an even harder time of it, Miss Mitsuko. You'd better come clean now, before it's too late." Seizing her by the lapels, Senkichi began to throttle her. "You see, it's getting worse already," he said. The bewildered look in her eyes made me laugh. In the end we untied her from the tree and pushed her to the ground, where she lay face up. "Look! A human bench!" I sat heavily on her lap, and Senkichi sat on her face. As we rocked this way and that, our buttocks pressed down on Mitsuko's body.

"Senkichi, stop," her muffled voice begged. "I'll tell the truth."

Lifting his bottom and slightly loosening his grip, he began his interrogation. "You promise? You *were* in the Western house a little while ago, weren't you?"

"Yes, I lied because I knew you'd ask me again to take you there. And if I took you, Mother would punish me."

Glaring at her, Senkichi said menacingly, "So, you won't take us? Here, it's going to hurt again."

"Ow! Ow! All right, I'll take you. I'll take you, so please stop. But let me take you at night, will you? If we go in the daytime, someone'll see us. I'll swipe the key from Torazō's room and open the door. Ei-chan, come back this evening if you want to go too."

Once she'd given in, we discussed our plans for the evening, while the two of us kept on pressing her to the ground. It happened to be the fifth of April, so I was to leave my house pretending to go to the monthly fair at Suitengū Shrine; when it got dark, I'd slip through the Hanawas' back gate to the entrance of the Western house, where Mitsuko, having stolen the key, would be waiting for me with Senkichi. If I were late, the two of them would go inside ahead of me and wait for me at the top of the stairs on the second floor, in the second room on the right.

"Okay, since we've settled that, I'll let you go. Get up." Senkichi finally released her.

"Ooh, that hurt. With you sitting on me, Senkichi, I couldn't breathe. And there was a big stone under my head." Mitsuko stood up, brushing the dust from her kimono and massaging her joints. Her cheeks and eyes were bright red, as though the blood had rushed to her head.

"What kinds of things are up there, anyway?" I asked, as I was about to leave for home.

"Lots of amazing things—you're in for a surprise." Smiling, she ran inside.

When I left the estate, I found that the lanterns on the stalls along Ningyō-chō Avenue had been lit, and the deep blasts of a conch shell signaling an exhibition of swordplay reverberated in the evening sky, as a large crowd of people milled about in front of Lord Arima's estate, with a medicine vendor expounding loudly as he pointed to a doll that depicted a woman's womb. I always looked forward to the seventy-five-piece shrine dances and Nagai Hyōsuke's displays of swordsmanship, but today neither of these held the slightest interest for me. I rushed home, took a bath, and hurried through dinner. It was perhaps seven o'clock when I raced out of the house again, crying, "I'm going to the fair!" The lights of the fair melted into the watery blue night air; the shadows of people dancing wildly on the second floor of the Kinseirō restaurant seemed close enough to touch; crowds of young men from the rice-traders' street, girls from the archery booths on the second block, and other men and women sauntered back and forth in droves along both sides of the street: this was the hour when the greatest number of people came out to see the sights. Crossing Nakanohashi Bridge to the gloomy, deserted streets of Hama-chō, I looked back to see the dark, thinly overcast sky stained a hazy red.

Before I knew it I stood before the Hanawas' house, looking up at the high black tiles that rose beyond like a mountain. A chilly breeze swept darkness along as it blew softly toward me from Shin-ōhashi Bridge, and the leaves of the giant zelkovas rustled somewhere in the sky. Peering into the enclosure, I saw only a thin, vertical beam of light escaping from a gap in the door to the porter's lodge. The main wing, all of its storm doors closed, lay like a sleeping demon, silent against the dull sky. Placing my hands on the cold steel grating of the service entrance beside the front gate, I pushed toward the darkness inside. The heavy door obediently creaked open. Walking softly so the soles of my leather sandals should make no sound, listening to my restless breathing and to the pounding of my heart, I moved forward, my eyes fixed on the glass door of the Western house, glowing in the dark.

Little by little, I could make things out in the darkness. Leaves of a *yatsude* shrub, zelkova branches, stone Kasuga lanterns—all sorts of dark objects, assuming postures to frighten a child's heart, forced their way into my sight. I sat on the granite steps, hanging my head in the penetrating stillness of the deepening night air, and held my breath as I waited, but the other two didn't come. The dread that hung over me set my body trembling, and my teeth chattered. *Oh, I should never have come to such a frightening place*, I told myself. Pressing my hands together, I blurted out a prayer: "I've been bad. I won't lie to Mother any more, or sneak into other people's houses."

Full of remorse, I stood up, intent on going back, but then, through the glass door at the entrance, I glimpsed what appeared to be the flame of a single, tiny candle. *Maybe the two of them went in ahead of me*, I thought. Suddenly the slave of curiosity again, I cast all discretion aside and placed my fingers on the doorknob. When I turned it, the door opened effortlessly.

Inside, just as I'd expected, I found a half-consumed candle at the foot of the spiral staircase before me, its soft wax trickling down the sides as it cast a feeble light about a yard in each direction. No doubt Mitsuko had left it there for me. In the air that followed me through the door, the flame flickered and swayed, and the shadow of the varnished stair rail shivered.

Holding my breath, I tiptoed like a burglar to the top of the spiral stairs, but the second-floor hallway was pitch-dark, there was no sign of anyone, nor was there the slightest sound. We'd agreed on the second door on the right. Groping my way, I edged up to it and strained my ears, but all was utter stillness. Filled half with fear and half with curiosity, I told myself I didn't care what happened, and pushed against the door with my shoulder.

A sudden ray of bright light pierced my eyes. Feeling dazed, I blinked and peered around the four walls, as if some phantom presence might be there, but I saw nothing of the kind. A large lamp hung in the center; its crimson shade, decorated with five-colored prisms, cast a shadow over the upper half of the room. Gold- and silver-inlaid tables, mirrors, and chairs and other ornaments shone brilliantly, and the softness of the deep-red carpet covering the floor felt pleasant through my socks, like fresh grass in a spring meadow.

"Mit-chan?" I wanted to call, but my surroundings were as desolate as if all life had become extinct. The solitude numbed my lips, stiffened my tongue, and robbed me of the courage to speak. At first I hadn't noticed, but in the far corner of the room, on the left, was the way into another room, with a heavy, deeply pleated damask curtain hanging across it like Niagara Falls. I pushed it aside and peered beyond, but my hands recoiled from the darkness behind the curtain. Just then a clock on the mantlepiece whirred like a cicada and began to play a queer, metallic music—*kin, kon, ken*. Thinking that this might be a cue for Mitsuko to make her entrance, I stared at the curtain, but two or three minutes passed, the music stopped, the room returned to its original stillness, and the damask pleats hung silent and motionless.

As I stood there blankly, I noticed an oil painting on the wall to the left. Moving absentmindedly toward the picture, I looked up at a half-length portrait of a Western girl, dimly shadowed by the lampshade. Within the thick, rectangular, gold frame floated a heavy, dark brown space, in the midst of which the girl—hair falling about her shoulders, breast lightly covered by a grayish blue robe, bare arms decorated with gold and gem-encrusted bracelets—stared straight ahead with dark, wide-open eyes, as if she were dreaming. The pure white of her skin, standing out vividly in the darkness, her beautiful, perfectly balanced features—the noble nose and lips, the chin, the cheeks: was this an angel from some fairy tale, I wondered as I looked up entranced. But just then my attention was caught by an ornamental snake on a table against the wall, a few feet below the picture. Whatever the snake was made of, it closely approached reality in the way it lifted its head like a fiddlehead above two coils and in the slippery blue-green of its scales. The more I looked at it, the more impressed I was, and I began to think it was about to move, when all at once I gasped and retreated two or three steps, my eyes riveted. Perhaps I had only imagined it, but the snake really seemed to be moving. In that extraordinarily sluggish way of reptiles, so deliberate that you'd miss it if you didn't watch closely, the snake was wriggling its head forward and backward, left and right. Feeling as cold as if I'd been doused with water, I paled and stood there petrified. Then the face of another girl, identical to the one in the oil painting, appeared between the pleats of the damask curtain.

The face smiled for a moment before the curtain parted, brushed against her shoulders, and closed again to form a backdrop for the girl who stood full-length before it.

The short, grayish blue skirt barely reached her knees. Below it she wore flesh-colored slippers on stockingless, alabaster feet; black hair spilled over her shoulders; her arms and throat were decorated with bracelets and necklaces, just as in the oil painting; and the movement of lithe muscles was visible through the garment that tightly bound her skin from breast to waist.

"Ei-chan." The moment she moved those lips—as red as if they held peony petals—I realized that the oil painting was a portrait of Mitsuko. ". . . I've been waiting for you." She moved slowly and menacingly to my side. An indescribably sweet aroma tickled my senses, a red haze flickered before my eyes.

"Are you alone, Mit-chan?" I asked nervously, in a voice that sounded like a call for help. There were lots of other questions I wanted to ask—why was she wearing Western clothing tonight, what was in that dark room next door?—but they caught in my throat and wouldn't come out.

"I'm going to show you Senkichi. Come with me."

I began to tremble when Mitsuko caught my wrist. "That snake is moving, isn't it?" I asked, beside myself with worry.

"Of course it isn't. Look," she smirked. Sure enough, the snake, which certainly had been moving before, now lay motionlessly coiled, not changing position in the least. "Stop looking at those things and come with me."

Mitsuko's warm, soft palm grasped my wrist lightly, but in an oddly compelling way that made it impossible to shake free, and pulled me toward the ominous room. Our bodies sank into the heavy damask curtain, and all too soon we were in that pitch-black chamber.

"Ei-chan, shall I let you see Senkichi?"

"Yes, where is he?"

"You'll know when I light a candle, just wait. . . . But first there's something fun I'm going to show you." Mitsuko released my wrist and disappeared. I heard a horrible snap in the darkness right in front of me. Countless fine white threads of light flew out, then began to race like meteors, writhe like waves, and describe circles and crosses.

"Isn't this fun? I can write anything at all." I heard Mitsuko's voice, and then she seemed to be at my side again. The threads of light gradually faded into darkness.

"What was that?"

"I scratched a foreign match against the wall. They catch fire wherever you scratch them. Shall I try lighting one on your kimono?"

"No, it's dangerous." Startled, I tried to get away.

"It's all right. Here, see?" Mitsuko casually pulled on the lapels of my kimono and struck a match. Glowing like a firefly crawling on the silk, a bluish green flame clearly drew the *katakana* letters *ha-gi-wa-ra*. They lingered there for a few moments.

"Now I'll light another and let you see Senkichi." With a crack, sparks flew as though Mitsuko had struck a flint against steel, a wax match flared up in her hand, and the flame moved to a candlestand in the center of the room.

In the dim illumination of the Western candle, assorted furnishings and ornaments cast big, long, black shadows on the four walls, where they ran rampant like evil spirits of the mountains, woods, streams, and rocks.

"Here's Senkichi." Mitsuko pointed beneath the candle. When I looked, I saw that what I'd thought was a candlestand was actually Senkichi, his hands and legs bound and his chest and arms bare as he sat looking up, a candle on his forehead. All over his face and head, the melting wax had flowed like bird droppings, threading over both eyes, covering his mouth, and dripping from the point of his chin into his lap. The flame of the candle, which was three-quarters consumed, seemed about to scorch his eyelashes, but he sat with his legs crossed like a Brahman ascetic, his fists tied behind him, quietly and correctly bearing up.

For some reason, as Mitsuko and I stood before him, Senkichi wriggled his jaw muscles under the wax that had stiffened his face, opened his eyes a crack, and glared at me reproachfully. Then in a heavy, cheerless voice he began to speak.

"You and I bullied her too much, so tonight she's taking her revenge. I'm already getting the full treatment. If you don't apologize fast, it'll be your turn. . . ."

Even as he spoke, the melting wax crept unimpeded, like worms, from his forehead to his lashes. He closed his eyes again and stiffened.

"Ei-chan, from now on don't listen to anything Shin-chan says, you're my slave, okay? If you say no, I'll have a bunch of snakes wrap themselves around you, like that statue over there."

With a menacing smile, Mitsuko pointed to an alabaster figurine on top of a bookcase filled with gold-lettered Western books. Raising my eyes fearfully toward the gloomy corner, I saw a sculpture of a muscular giant wrapped in pythons and making a dreadful face. Beside it two or three blue-green snakes, just like that other one, were calmly coiled in waiting, like incense burners; but, only conscious of the horror they aroused, I couldn't be sure whether they were real snakes or imitations.

"You'll do anything I say, won't you?"

Ashen-faced, I nodded silently.

"The other day you and Senkichi used me as a bench, so now *you* can be a candlestand." Mitsuko promptly tied my hands behind me, had me sit cross-legged beside Senkichi, and firmly bound my ankles. "Look up so you won't drop the candle," she said, lighting one in the center of my forehead. Unable to speak, I struggled to support the flame as tears trickled down my cheeks. Presently the melting wax, hotter even than my tears, came dripping across my brow and covered my eyes and mouth; but through the thin skin of my eyelids I could vaguely see the candle's flicker. My vision faded into a red blur, and the scent of Mitsuko's rich perfume showered down onto my face.

"I want the two of you to stay like that for a little longer. I'm going to let you hear something nice." With that, Mitsuko went away, but presently the void was broken by the mysterious resonance of the piano, issuing from the stillness of the next room.

The strange sounds, now like hailstones rolling on a silver platter, now like springwater trickling over moss in a ravine, came to my ears as sounds from another world. The candle on my forehead must have burned very short, as hot perspiration, mingled with wax, began to flow in dribbles. I glanced sideways at Senkichi sitting beside me: white lumps clung to his face like so much wheat flour, piled up to a thickness of a quarter-inch or more, so that he looked like burdock tempura. We sat there entranced by the delicate music, like the people in the story of the merry violin, gazing endlessly at the bright world beneath our eyelids.

From the next day on, Senkichi and I fell to our knees as limp as cats whenever her presence required it. If Shin'ichi ever tried to go against his sister he'd promptly find himself being tied up or pummeled by us two. Thus in the course of time even this haughty character became one of Mitsuko's minions, utterly transformed at home into the same servile mollycoddle that he'd always been at school. All three of us cheerfully obeyed Mitsuko's commands as though we'd discovered some marvelous new game. If she said "Stools," we'd drop to our hands and knees and yield up our backs; if she said

"Spittoons," we'd sit up formally and open our mouths. As she grew increasingly willful, Mitsuko would drive us like slaves and keep us always in attendance at her side, making us trim her nails after the bath, ordering us to clean her nostrils, and giving us pee to drink. For a long time she reigned over us like a queen.

I never went into the Western house again. As for those blue-green snakes, even now I'm not sure whether they were real or artificial.

The Secret

TRANSLATED BY
Anthony H. Chambers

On a whim I withdrew from the lively scene around me, slipped away from the circle of men and women with whom I'd maintained a variety of relationships, and finally, after searching for an appropriate hideaway, found a monastery run by the Shingon sect in the Matsuba-chō district of Asakusa, where I rented a room in the monks' quarters.

The monastery was in an obscure, labyrinthine neighborhood in the shadow of the Twelve-Story Tower, reached by following the Shinbori Canal in a straight line from Kikuya Bridge and behind the Honganji Temple. The slum spread over the district like an overturned trash bin, and along one edge of it stretched the ocher earthen wall that surrounded the monastery. The enclosure gave an impression of great calm, gravity, and solitude.

Rather than secluding myself in a suburb like Shibuya or Ōkubo, I thought from the outset that somewhere in the central city I could surely find some secret, timeworn place, unnoticed by anyone else. Just as stagnant pools form here and there in a swift mountain stream, secluded pockets must lie between the bustling streets in the heart of the city—quiet sections through which most people would never have occasion to pass.

There were other considerations as well.

An enthusiastic traveler, I'd been to Kyoto and Sendai and from Hokkaido in the north to Kyushu in the south, but right here in

Tokyo—where I'd lived for twenty years since my birth in Ningyō-chō—there probably were streets on which I'd never set foot. Indeed, there must have been many of them. In the honeycomb of streets wide and narrow at the heart of this huge city, I could no longer be certain which were more numerous—those I'd passed down or those I hadn't.

I must have been eleven or twelve years old when I went with my father to the Hachiman Shrine in Fukagawa.

"Now we'll take the ferry and I'll treat you to the famous noodles at Komeichi in Fuyugi," he said, leading me around behind the shrine buildings. The narrow, brimming, low-banked river, so unlike the canals at Koami-chō or Kobuna-chō, pushed its languid way between the eaves of houses packed together on either side. Weaving between the barges and lighters that floated parallel to the banks and looked longer than the channel was wide, the little ferry crossed back and forth with only two or three strokes of the pole against the bottom.

I'd often visited the Hachiman Shrine before, but I never gave any thought to what might lie behind the compound. I always paid my respects to the main building from the direction of the *torii* gate in front, and so I suppose I simply thought of it as a flat, dead-end view, all front and no back, like a panoramic picture. Now as I gazed at the river and the ferry and the land stretching forever beyond them, the unfamiliar scene reminded me of the worlds one often encounters in dreams, far more remote from Tokyo than either Kyoto or Osaka.

I tried to picture the streets behind the Kannon Hall at Asakusa, but nothing came to mind except the tiled roof of the massive red building itself, seen from the line of shops leading up to it. As I grew older and my contacts expanded, I felt as though I'd explored every corner of Tokyo in the course of visiting friends, going to see the cherry blossoms, and other outings, but often enough I would stumble on hidden enclaves like those I'd discovered as a child.

I searched high and low, thinking that a world set apart like that would be the ideal place to hide, and the more I explored, the more neighborhoods I found through which I'd never passed before. I had crossed Asakusa Bridge and Izumi Bridge many times, but I'd never set foot on Saemon Bridge, which lies in between. Going to the Ichimuraza Theater in Nichō-chō, I'd always turn at the corner by the noodle shop, from the avenue where the trolley runs; but I couldn't recall ever having walked the two or three blocks beyond the theater, toward the Ryūseiza. What was the east bank like to the left of the old Eitai Bridge? I couldn't be sure. The neighborhoods around Echizenbori, Shamisenbori, and San'yabori were also unfamiliar to me.

The monastery at Matsuba-chō was in the strangest neighborhood of all. Just around the corner and down the alley from the Rokku amusement district and the Yoshiwara licensed quarter, this lonely, forgotten section delighted me. It was fun to leave behind that old friend of mine—"gaudy, extravagant, commonplace Tokyo"—and be able to watch the commotion quietly from my hiding place.

I didn't go into seclusion to study. My nerves in those days were worn smooth, like an old file, and responded only to the most vivid, full-bodied stimuli. I could no longer enjoy first-rate art or food that required a delicate sensibility. I felt too jaded to respond to the ordinary urban pleasures, to appreciate a chef in the gay quarters—the embodiment of the smart, downtown style—or to admire the skill of kabuki actors from western Japan, like Nizaemon and Ganjirō. The predictable and indolent life I'd been leading from force of habit, day after day, was now more than I could bear. I wanted to try a more unconventional, fanciful, artificial mode of life.

Was there nothing weird and mysterious enough to make my deadened nerves shudder with excitement? Was there nowhere I could indulge in a barbaric, fantastical atmosphere, closer to a dream-world than reality? I let my mind wander through the realms of ancient Babylonian and Assyrian legends, recalled the detective stories of Conan Doyle and Ruikō, longed for the burned earth and green fields of the tropics, where the sun's rays are so intense, and looked back fondly on the eccentric mischief of my childhood.

I thought that dropping out of sight and willfully keeping my activities secret would be enough to provide my life with a certain mysterious, romantic quality. I'd savored the pleasures of secrets since childhood. The pleasure of games like hide-and-seek, treasure hunt, and blindman's buff—especially on a dark evening, in a dimly lit storeroom, or before the double-leafed storehouse doors—came primarily from the aura of secrecy inherent in them. It was from a desire to experience again the sensations I'd enjoyed as a child playing hide-and-seek that I hid myself downtown in that obscure, unnoticed spot. Also, the monastery's affiliation with the esoteric Shingon sect, intimately associated with secrets, charms, maledictions, and the like, was calculated to appeal to my curiosity and to foster my daydreams.

My room was in a newly enlarged section of the living quarters. It faced south, and the eight floor mats had been slightly discolored by the sun, imparting a rather peaceful, warm feeling to the room. In the afternoon, when the gentle autumn sun blazed red like a magic lantern against the *shōji* by the veranda, the room was as bright as a paper-covered lampstand.

Shelving the documents on philosophy and art that had been my companions until then, I littered the room with books rich in weird tales and illustrations—detective novels, books on magic, hypnotism, chemistry, and anatomy, which I'd take up at random and immerse myself in as I lay sprawled on the mats. Among them were Conan Doyle's *The Sign of Four*, De Quincey's *Murder, Considered as One of the Fine Arts*, tales like *The Arabian Nights*, and even a strange French book on "sexologie."

I prevailed upon the head priest to lend me old Buddhist paintings of Hell and Paradise, Mt. Sumeru, and the recumbent Buddha from his private collection. These I hung haphazardly on the walls of my room, like maps on the walls of the teachers' room at school. A steady thread of mauve smoke rose calmly from the incense burner in the alcove and filled the bright, warm room with its fragrance. Now and then I'd go to a shop beside Kikuya Bridge and buy some sandalwood or aloes to put in the burner.

The room presented a mesmerizing spectacle on clear days, when the rays of the noontime sun struck the *shōji* with full force. From the old paintings that covered the surrounding walls, brilliantly colored Buddhas, *arhats, bhiksu, bhiksuni, upāsaka, upāsikā*, elephants, lions, and unicorns swam out into the abundant light to join a host of living figures from the countless books thrown open on the floor— on manslaughter, anesthesia, narcotics, witchcraft, religion—merging with the incense smoke and looming dimly over me as I lay on a small scarlet rug, gazing with the glassy eyes of a savage, conjuring up hallucinations, day after day.

At about nine o'clock in the evening, after the other residents of the monastery were fast asleep, I'd get drunk by gulping down some whiskey from a square bottle. Then I'd slide open the wooden shutters at the veranda, climb over the graveyard hedge, and set out for a walk. Changing my costume every night so as not to be recognized, I plunged into the crowd in Asakusa Park or picked through the shop-front displays of antique dealers and secondhand bookstores. One night I'd tie a scarf over my head, don a short cotton coat with vertical stripes, apply red polish to the nails of my carefully scrubbed bare feet, and slip on leather-soled sandals. Another night I might go out wearing gold-rimmed dark glasses and an Inverness with the collar turned up. I enjoyed using a false beard, a mole, or a birthmark to alter my features. But one night, at a secondhand clothing shop in Shamisenbori, I saw a woman's lined kimono with a delicate speckled pattern against a blue ground, and was seized with a desire to try it on.

When it came to clothing and fabric, I felt a deep, keen interest which went beyond a simple liking for a good color combination or a stylish design. Whenever I saw or touched a beautiful piece of silk, I wanted to wrap my body in it. Often the pleasure it gave rose up inside me to a crest, as if I were gazing at the texture of a lover's skin. And though it wasn't only women's garments that attracted me, I did sometimes feel jealous of women, whose lot permitted them to wear, without embarrassment and whenever they wanted, the silk crepes I loved so much.

The idea of wearing that fine-patterned crepe kimono, languid and fresh in the secondhand clothing shop—the delicious sensation of that soft, heavy, cool fabric clinging to my flesh—made me shiver with anticipation. *I want to put it on*, I told myself. *I want to walk the streets dressed as a woman.* Without a second thought, I decided to buy it. I even bought a long Yūzen underkimono and a black crepe jacket to go with it.

The kimono must once have been worn by a large woman, because it was just the right size for a smallish man like me. As the night darkened and silence fell over the big, empty monastery, I took my place stealthily before the mirror and began to apply my makeup. The effect was a bit grotesque at first, when I smeared some white paste on the yellow skin at the bridge of my nose; but when I used my palms to extend the thick white liquid to every part of my face, it spread surprisingly well, and the sensation of that sweetly fragrant, cool dew seeping into my pores was invigorating. When I applied rouge and polishing powder, I was delighted at the transformation of my alabaster-white face into that of a fresh, animated-looking woman. It made me realize that the techniques of makeup, tested every day by actors, geisha, and ordinary women on their own bodies, are far more interesting than the arts of the painter or the man of letters.

Long underkimono, detachable collar, underskirt, rustling sleeves lined with red silk—my flesh was granted the same sensations as those known by the skin of every woman. I whitened my wrists and the nape of my neck, donned a wig in the gingko-leaf style, covered my head and mouth with a hood, and ventured out into the night streets.

It was a dark evening and the sky looked like rain. I wandered for a while in the lonely streets of Senzoku-chō, Kiyosumi-chō, and Ryūsenji-chō, all laced with canals, but neither the policemen on beat nor any passerby seemed to notice me. The cool touch of the night wind made my face feel dry, as though an extra layer of skin had been stretched over it. The hood over my mouth grew warm and moist from my breath, and at every step the hems of my long crepe underskirt tangled playfully with my legs. Thanks to the waistband binding my pelvis and the wide sash wrapped tightly from the pit of my stomach to my ribs, I felt as though feminine blood had naturally begun to flow in my veins, and masculine feelings and postures gradually disappeared.

When I extended my white-painted hands from the shadow of my Yūzen sleeves, their firm, sturdy lines faded in the darkness, and they floated there softly, white and plump. I loved the way they looked; I envied women for having beautiful hands like these. What fun it would be to dress like this and commit all sorts of crimes, like Ben-ten Kozō on the stage! Sharing something of the mood of secrecy and suspicion that readers of detective novels and crime stories appreciate, I gradually turned my steps toward the crowded Rokku section of the park. It wasn't hard to imagine I was someone who'd committed a particularly brutal crime, perhaps murder, or robbery.

When I went from the Twelve-Story Tower to the bank of the

pond, and then to the intersection by the Opera House, decorative lighting and arc lamps glittered on my heavily made-up face and brought out the colors and pattern on my kimono. Arriving in front of the Tokiwaza Theater, I saw myself reflected in a giant mirror at the entrance to a photographer's studio, splendidly transformed into a woman among the bustling throng.

Under my thick white makeup, the secret man was hidden completely—my eyes and mouth moved like a woman's, seemed on the point of smiling like a woman's. None of the many women who passed me in the crowd, giving off the sweet smell of camphor and the faint rustle of silk, ever doubted that I was one of their own species. Among them were some who looked enviously at the elegance with which I'd made up my face, and at my old-style clothing.

Everything about the familiar night-time commotion in the park looked new in the light of this disguise. Everywhere I went, everything I saw was as rare and curious as something encountered for the first time. Ordinary reality seemed to be endowed with a dreamlike mystery when I viewed it from behind a veil of secrecy, deceiving human eyes and electric lights under the cover of voluptuous cosmetics and crepe garments.

From that time on, I continued this masquerade almost every night, growing confident enough to mingle in the gallery of the Miyatoza Theater and in motion-picture houses. It would be close to midnight when I returned to the monastery, but as soon as I went inside I'd light the oil lamp, sprawl on the rug without loosening the clothing on my tired body, and gaze with lingering regret at the colors of my gorgeous kimono as I waved the sleeves back and forth. When I faced the mirror, the white powder had begun to wear thin but was still clinging to the coarse skin on my sagging cheeks. As I stared at the image, a degenerate pleasure, like the intoxication of old wine, stirred my soul. With the paintings of Hell and Paradise behind me,

I'd sometimes recline languidly on my quilts like a courtesan, still wearing my showy long underkimono, and flip through the pages of weird volumes until dawn. As I grew more daring and more skilled in disguise, I'd slip a knife or an opiate into the folds of my sash before I went out, the better to excite fanciful associations. Without committing any crime, I wanted fully to inhale the romantic fragrance attendant on crime.

Then, one evening about a week later, thanks to a strange concurrence, I stumbled upon the makings of an even weirder, more fanciful, and more disturbing affair.

That evening, having drunk a good deal more whiskey than usual, I went up to the special reserved seats on the second floor of the San'yūkan movie house. It must have been close to ten o'clock. The packed theater was heavy with thick, smoky air, and the smell of humanity rose warmly from the silent, squirming crowd below to float about me, threatening to spoil my makeup. With each sharp squeak of the projector in the darkness, and each ray of light piercing my eyes from the dizzily unfolding movie, my drunken head hurt as if it would split. Now and then the movie would stop and the electric lights would go on suddenly, and I'd look around from the deep shadow of my hood, through the tobacco smoke that drifted over the heads of the crowd downstairs like clouds rising from a valley floor, at the faces of the people who overflowed the theater. I took secret pride in the fact that many men were peering curiously at my old-fashioned hood, and many women stealing covetous glances at the smart hues of my clothing. In novelty of dress, seductiveness, and beauty, none of the women in the audience was as conspicuous as I was.

At first no one sat next to me. I don't know exactly when the seats came to be occupied, but when the lights went on for the second or third time, I realized that a man and a woman were sitting just to my left.

The woman looked twenty-two or -three, but in fact was probably four or five years older than that. Her hair was done smartly in the *mitsuwa* style, and her entire body was wrapped in an azure silk-crepe manteau; only her lovely face, which glowed with health, was clearly, even ostentatiously, exposed. Something about her made it difficult to know whether she was a geisha or an unmarried young lady, but it was apparent from the attitude of the gentleman with her that she wasn't a respectable married woman.

". . . Arrested at last. . . ." In a low voice she read out an English title that appeared on the screen. Blowing richly fragrant smoke from an M.C.C. Turkish cigarette into my face, she threw me a sparkling glance with her big eyes, eyes that gleamed more sharply in the dark than the jewel on her finger.

It was a husky voice, like that of a professional balladeer, out of keeping with her charming figure—unmistakably the voice of a woman called T. with whom I'd formed a casual, shipboard relationship when I'd traveled to Shanghai two or three years before.

In those days, too, I recalled, I couldn't tell from her manner and dress whether she was a professional woman or a respectable lady. The man who accompanied her on the ship and the man with her tonight were quite different in bearing and features; but no doubt there were countless men running like a chain through the woman's past, linking the gap between these two men. In any case, she was clearly the sort of person who flits like a butterfly from man to man.

Two years earlier, she had fallen in love with me on that sea voyage, but we reached Shanghai without having exchanged our real names or any information about ourselves, and, once there, I casually dropped her and slipped out of sight. I'd thought of her simply as a woman in a dream on the Pacific Ocean; I never expected to see her again, particularly in a place like this. She'd been a little plump before, but now she was wonderfully slender and sleek, and her round, moist eyes, with their long eyelashes, were limpid and imperious enough to make a man doubt that he was man enough. Only her lips—so fresh in color that one would think they might leave a crimson bloodstain on whatever they touched—and the length of the hair at the side of her face were unchanged. Her nose appeared to be higher and sharper than before.

Had she noticed me? I couldn't be certain. When the lights went on, I guessed from the way she was flirting in whispers with her companion that she'd dismissed me as an ordinary woman and was paying me no particular attention. The only certainty was that, sitting next to her, I couldn't help feeling ashamed of the costume I'd been so proud of. Overawed by the charm of this vital, seductive creature, I felt like a freak in the makeup and clothing I'd taken so much trouble over. Unable to compete with her in femininity or in beauty, I faded away, like a star before the moon.

How pretty her supple, fluttering hand was, swimming like a fish from the shadow of her manteau, clearly defined in the murky air that hung so densely in the theater. Even as she was speaking with the man, she'd raise her eyes dreamily and look at the ceiling, knit her brows and look down at the crowd, or show her white teeth as she laughed, and her face would brim with a different expression each time. Her large black eyes, capable apparently of expressing virtually any meaning, were being scrutinized like jewels from even the furthest recesses of the ground floor. The parts of which her face was made were too suggestive to be mere organs for seeing, smelling, hearing, or speaking; too sweet to be anything but the sugared bait by which to catch a man's heart.

No one's gaze was directed at me now. Like a fool, I began to feel jealousy and rage over the beauty of the woman who'd usurped my popularity. It was mortifying to be slighted, to have my own light extinguished by the charming features of a woman I'd once toyed with and abandoned. Perhaps she'd recognized me after all and was taking her ironic revenge.

Gradually, though, I sensed my jealousy of her looks change to longing. Defeated as a woman, I wanted to win her over again as a man, and to revel in the victory. I was seized by an urge to grab hold of that supple body and crush it in my arms.

> *Do you know who I am? Seeing you tonight after all this time, I am falling in love with you again. If you feel you might like to link up with me again, could you come and wait for me in these seats again tomorrow evening? I would prefer not to let anyone know my address, and so beg you to come here tomorrow at the same hour and wait for me.*

Under cover of darkness I took a piece of Japanese paper and a pencil from my sash, dashed off this note, and slipped it into her sleeve; I then watched her carefully.

She calmly saw the movie through until it ended at around eleven o'clock. Then, taking advantage of the confusion when the audience rose and began noisily to disperse, she whispered in my ear, ". . . Arrested at last. . . ." She gazed at my face for a moment with even more confidence and daring than before, and finally disappeared with her companion into the crowd.

". . . Arrested at last. . . ."

She had recognized me. The thought made me shudder.

But would she come as requested the following night? She seemed far more worldly than before. Had I underestimated her and given her the advantage? Tense with anxiety and trepidation, I returned to the monastery.

There, as usual, I was just removing my outer garments so that I'd be dressed only in my long underkimono, when a small piece of

Western paper, folded into a square, fell from inside my hood.

"Mr. S. K." The ink inscription shone like silk when I held it up to the light. It was unmistakably her handwriting. She'd stepped out once or twice during the film—in the interval she must have penned an answer quickly and slipped it into my collar without anyone noticing.

I never dreamed I'd see you here of all places. You may have changed your clothing, but how could I fail to recognize the face I've never forgotten these three years, even in my dreams? I knew from the beginning that the woman in the hood was you. I find it amusing, by the way, to see that you're as eccentric as ever. At the same time, it makes me uneasy to think that you may simply be indulging this eccentricity when you say that you want to meet me, but I'm too happy to be able to judge properly, so I shall do as you say and wait for you tomorrow night without fail. For reasons of my own, however, I wonder if you would mind going to the Thunder Gate crossing between nine and nine-thirty. A rickshaw man whom I shall send to meet you will pick you up and take you to my house. Just as you want to conceal your address, I, too, prefer that you not know where I live, and so I shall arrange for the man to bring you to me blindfolded. I hope that you will agree to this one condition, because if you don't, I shall never be able to see you again, and nothing could be sadder than that.

As I read this letter, I felt that I'd become a character in a detective story. Curiosity and alarm both swirled around in my head. Maybe the woman understood my own proclivities so well that she was acting like this deliberately.

There was a heavy downpour the next evening. Changing my costume completely, I put on a man's silk kimono and a mackintosh and went splashing into the night. The rain pounded on my silk umbrella like a waterfall. The Shinbori Canal having overflowed into the surrounding streets, I tucked my *tabi* socks into the breast of my kimono and walked on my clogs barefoot. My feet glistened in the lamplight that spilled from the houses along the street. Everything was blotted out by the din of the driving rain; most of the shutters were closed on the usually bustling avenues, and two or three men with their skirts tucked up ran off like routed soldiers. Aside from an occasional trolley spraying puddles of water from the rails as it passed, there were only the lamps placed here and there above utility-pole advertisements, dimly illuminating the hazy, rain-filled air.

When I finally reached the Thunder Gate crossing, my mackintosh, my wrists, and even my elbows were soaking wet. Standing dejectedly in the rain, I looked around in the light from the arc lamps, but no one was in sight. Perhaps someone was hiding in a dark corner and keeping an eye on me. I stood there for a time with this thought in mind, until finally, in the darkness toward Azuma Bridge, I saw a red lantern moving along, and an old-fashioned, two-passenger rickshaw rattled swiftly across the paving stones by the trolley tracks and came to a stop before me.

The rickshaw man was wearing a large, round wicker hat and a rain cape. "Please get in, sir." As his voice melted in the drumming of the rain, he moved quickly around behind me, wrapped a length of fine silk twice around my eyes, and pulled it so tight that it pinched the skin at my temples.

"Here, let's get in." The man grasped me with his rough hands and lifted me into the rickshaw.

The rain beat against the musty canvas hood. It was clear that a woman was riding beside me. Inside the hood, the air was stuffy with body heat and the smell of white makeup.

Lifting the rickshaw's shaft, the man spun us around several times in the same spot to mask the direction in which he finally started off. Before long he turned right, then left. It felt as though we were wandering in a labyrinth. Now and then we entered a street with a trolley line or crossed a little bridge.

We were rocked by the rickshaw for a long time. The woman beside me must of course have been T., but she sat there without speaking or moving. No doubt she was riding with me to make sure that I kept my blindfold on. Even without her supervision, though, I would have had no desire to remove it. The dream-woman I'd met at sea, the interior of a rickshaw on a rainy evening, the secrets of the city at night, blindness, silence—all these had merged to plunge me into the haze of a perfect mystery.

Presently the woman parted my tight lips and put a cigarette in my mouth. Striking a match, she lit it for me.

After about an hour, the rickshaw finally stopped. Taking hold of me again with his rough hands, the man guided me fifteen or twenty feet down what seemed to be a narrow alley, opened what must have been a back door, and led me into a house.

Left in a room with my eyes still covered, I sat alone for a while. Before long I heard the sound of a sliding door being opened. Without saying a word, the woman snuggled up to me, her body as limp and fluid as a mermaid's. She lay back on my lap, put her arms around my neck, and untied my blindfold.

The room was about eight mats in size, or twelve feet by twelve. The construction and furnishings were excellent and the wood well chosen, but just as the woman's status was unclear, I couldn't tell whether it was a house of assignation, a kept-woman's home, or a respectable, upper-class residence. Beyond the veranda was some thick shrubbery, enclosed by a wooden fence. Given only this range of vision, I couldn't begin to guess what part of Tokyo the house might be in.

"I'm so glad you came," the woman said, leaning against a square rosewood table in the center of the room and letting her white arms creep languidly on its surface like two living creatures. I was astonished by the tremendous change in her appearance from the night before—she was wearing an austere, striped kimono with a removable collar and a lined sash, and her hair was done in the everyday, ginkgo-leaf style.

"You must think it odd that I'm dressed like this tonight. But the only way to keep others from knowing one's circumstances is to alter one's appearance every day." As she spoke, she lifted a cup from the table and poured some wine into it. Her manner was more gentle and subdued than I remembered.

"I'm glad you haven't forgotten me. Since we parted company in Shanghai, I've known all sorts of men and suffered as a result, but, strangely, I couldn't forget you. Please don't drop me like that again. Go on meeting me—forever—as someone whose position and circumstances you don't know. A dream-woman."

Every word and phrase left a sad little echo in me, like music from some strange land. How could the flashy, spirited, intelligent woman of the night before present such a melancholy, admirable figure tonight? It was as if she'd discarded everything and was now baring her soul to me.

"Dream-woman," "secret woman"—savoring this strange liaison, in which the distinction between reality and illusion was always blurred, I went to her house almost every night and enjoyed myself there until two o'clock in the morning, when, blindfolded again, I'd be escorted back to the Thunder Gate crossing. We met for a month, then two months, without knowing each other's address or name. At first I had no desire to investigate her circumstances or seek out her residence; but as the days passed, I was moved by a strange curiosity—what part of Tokyo was the rickshaw carrying us to? How did we get from Asakusa to here, the neighborhood I was passing through now with my eyes covered? I was determined to know this much. Maybe the woman's house, where the rickshaw finally came to rest after thirty minutes, an hour, sometimes an hour and a half of rattling through the city streets, was surprisingly close to the Thunder Gate crossing. As I was rocked along every night in the rickshaw, I couldn't help speculating secretly about our location .

One night I could stand it no longer. "Take off this blindfold, won't you?" I pleaded with the woman while we were in the rickshaw. "Just for a moment."

"No, no, you mustn't!" She gripped my hands in panic and pressed her face against them. "Please, don't be difficult. This route is my secret. You might stop seeing me if you discovered it."

"Why would I do that?"

"Because I'd no longer be a 'dream-woman.' You love the woman in the dream more than you love me."

I tried everything I could think of to overcome her reluctance.

"I have no choice, then," she finally said with a sigh. "I'll let you look . . . but only for a moment." With obvious misgivings, she removed my blindfold. "Can you tell where we are now?" she asked uneasily.

Against an unusually black sky, stars glittered everywhere in the wonderfully clear air, and the white mist of the Milky Way flowed from one horizon to the other. The narrow street, lined with shops on both sides, was gaily illuminated by lamplight. The lane was a lively one, but oddly enough I had no idea where it was. The rickshaw ran on down the street until the name "Seibidō," written in large letters on a seal-maker's shop sign, came into view at the end of the street, a block or two ahead.

When I peered from the rickshaw at the small lettering at the edge of the sign where the shop's address was written, the woman seemed suddenly to notice. "Oh, no," she said, and covered my eyes again.

A busy little street with many shops and a seal-maker's sign at the end—I decided it must be a street I'd never traveled along before.

Once again I felt the tug of curiosity I'd felt as a child when confronted with a riddle.

"Could you make out the letters on that sign?"

"No, I couldn't. I have no idea where we are. And I know nothing about your life, except what happened three years ago on the Pacific. It's as if you put a spell on me, and whisked me off to some phantom land a thousand leagues away."

Hearing my reply, the woman said in a poignant voice, "I hope you'll always feel that way. Think of me as a woman in a dream who lives in a phantom land. Please, never insist again the way you did just now."

I guessed that there were tears in her eyes.

For some time after that, I couldn't forget the mysterious street scene I'd been allowed to glimpse that evening. The seal-maker's sign at the end of that busy, brightly lit lane was etched sharply in my mind. I racked my brains trying to think of a way to find that street, until finally I worked out a plan.

In the course of those long months when we were being pulled around together nearly every night, the number of revolutions the rickshaw made at the Thunder Gate crossing and the number of right and left turns settled into a routine, and before I knew it I'd memorized the pattern. One morning I stood on a corner at the crossing and, with my eyes closed, turned myself around several times. When I thought I had it about right, I trotted off at the same pace as a rickshaw. My only method was to calculate the intervals as best I could and turn into side streets here and there. Sure enough, there was a bridge, and there was a street with trolley rails, just where they should be; and so I thought I must be on the right track.

The route, beginning at the Thunder Gate crossing, skirted the edge of the park as far as Senzoku-chō and followed a narrow lane through Ryūsenji-chō toward Ueno. At Kurumazaka-shita it bore to the left and, after following the Okachimachi street for seven or eight blocks, once again turned to the left. Here I ran smack into the narrow street I'd seen that night.

And right in front of me was the seal-maker's sign.

Keeping my eyes on the sign, I advanced straight forward, as though I were probing the inner depths of a secret cavern. When I reached the end of the street and looked at the cross street, I was surprised to see that it was a continuation of the Shitaya Take-chō avenue, where a bazaar is held every evening. Just a few yards away, I could see the secondhand clothing shop where I'd bought that fine-patterned crepe kimono. The mysterious lane connected Shamisen-bori and the Naka-Okachimachi street, but I couldn't recall ever having passed through it before. I stood for a while in front of the Seibidō sign that had puzzled me for so long. The houses lining the street had been crowned that night by a sky full of dazzling stars, wrapped in a dreamlike, mysterious air, and brimming with red lamps; but now they looked like shacks, shriveled in the hot rays of the autumn sun. I felt immediately disappointed.

Spurred on by an irrepressible curiosity, though, I guessed at the direction and ran on, like a dog returning to its home, following a scent on the road.

When I entered Asakusa Ward again, the route proceeded to the right from Kojima-chō, crossed a street with a trolley line near Suga Bridge, followed the bank of the Daichi River toward Yanagi Bridge, and emerged at the avenue leading to Ryōgoku. I could see what a roundabout way the woman had taken to make me lose my bearings. I passed Yagenbori, Hisamatsu-chō, Hama-chō, and crossed Kakihama Bridge—and suddenly I didn't know which way to go.

I was sure that the woman's house was in an alley nearby. I spent an hour going in and out of narrow side streets in the neighborhood.

Directly across from the Dōryō Gongen temple, in a narrow space between the eaves of the tightly packed houses, I found a humble, narrow, nearly invisible alley. Intuitively I knew that the woman's house lay down that alley. I went in. The second or third house on the right was enclosed by a handsome wooden fence which had been treated to bring out the grain, and from the railing of a second-floor window, through a screen of pine needles, the woman was staring down at me with an ashen face.

Unable to hide the mocking look in my eyes, I gazed up at the second floor, but the woman returned my stare expressionlessly, as though she were feigning ignorance and pretending to be someone else. Indeed, she might as well have been disguised as someone else, so different was her appearance now from the impression she'd given at night. She had agreed, just once, to a man's request to loosen his blindfold; but that had been enough for her secret to be exposed. A trace of the regret and sadness she must have felt showed fleetingly on her face, and then, without a sound, she disappeared behind the *shōji*.

Her name was Yoshino. She was a widow, and wealthy for that neighborhood. As with the seal-maker's sign, all her riddles had been solved. I stopped seeing her at once.

Two or three days later I left the monastery and moved to Tabata. The satisfactions to be gained from "secrets" were now too bland and pallid for me. I intended to seek more vivid, gory pleasures.

THE $\mathcal{T}$wo Acolytes

TRANSLATED BY
Paul McCarthy

The two acolytes were only two years apart in age—thirteen and fifteen. The elder was called Senjumaru, the younger Rurikōmaru. Each had been entrusted by his parents at an early age to Mt. Hiei, the great Buddhist monastery to the northeast of the capital, where no women were permitted access. There, an eminent monk took charge of the two boys' upbringing. Senjumaru had been born into a prosperous family in the province of Ōmi, but circumstances arose that led to his being brought to the monastery when he was four. Rurikōmaru was actually the son of a Lesser Councillor at the Imperial Court; but he too, for certain reasons, was taken to the holy mountain—the spiritual protector of the imperial capital—at the tender age of three, soon after being weaned from his wet nurse's breast. Of course, neither of the boys had any clear memory of what had happened, nor any reliable evidence of their own families; there was merely talk and rumors from here and there. They had neither father nor mother, only the monk who had so carefully reared them. They relied on him as a parent, and felt sure it was their destiny to enter the Way of the Buddha.

"You should regard yourselves as very lucky boys. If ordinary people yearn for their parents and long for their hometowns, it's all the result of worldly passions and karmic attachments. But you two have known nothing of the world beyond this holy mountain and have no parents, so you're free of the suffering that comes from worldly passions." The monk often told them this, and indeed they felt grateful for their situation. Why, even the good holy man himself, before retreating to Mt. Hiei, had known the pangs of all kinds of desire in the world outside. He had engaged in meditation for a very long time before he was able finally to cut the bonds of attachment, it was said. And there were many among his present disciples who, though they listened to his lectures on the sutras each morning and evening, were still unable to conquer their passions, and mourned the fact. But the two of them, not knowing anything of the world, had been immune to the dreadful sickness of desire. They had learned that, once the passions were overcome, the fruit of enlightenment was one's eventual reward. And here they were, free from those temptations from the very start! They eagerly looked forward to having their hair shaved off and taking the precepts of a monk, and in due course becoming true followers of the Way, just like their teacher. They were sure of it, and spent their days in that hope.

Nonetheless, they had a certain innocent curiosity about the perilous outside world of passion and pain. Neither ever wanted actually to try living in such a sinful place, but they did think about it and imagine it from time to time. Their teacher and other elders told them that, of all the places in the defiled world, only the holy mountain where they now were gave some hint of the glories of the Pure Land to the West. The vast expanse of land stretching in all directions from the foothills of the holy mountain beneath the blue sky dappled with white clouds—that was the world of the five defilements so vividly described in the sutras. The two of them would stand on the top of Mt. Shimei and look down toward where, as they'd been told, their old homes were; they couldn't help fantasizing, indulging in childish dreams.

One day Senjumaru, gazing toward the province of Ōmi, pointed at Lake Biwa shining beneath a faint purple haze and said to Rurikōmaru in the confident manner of an elder brother to a younger,

"Well, that's the 'fleeting world' everybody talks about, but what do you suppose it's really like?"

"They say it's a horrible place, full of dust and dirt, but when you look at it from here, the surface of that lake looks as clear as a mirror. Doesn't it seem that way to you too?" said Rurikōmaru a bit timidly, as if afraid of being laughed at by his older friend for saying something stupid.

"Oh, but under the surface of that beautiful lake lives a dragon god, and on Mt. Mikami on the shore there's a giant centipede that's even bigger than that dragon! I'll bet you didn't know that. The world outside looks very pretty from up here, but if you once go down, you'd better be careful! That's what our Master says, and I'm sure he's right." A knowing smile played about Senjumaru's lips.

Another time Rurikōmaru was looking at the sky over the distant capital. He pointed at the ripples of gray rooftiles there in the lowlands, spread out before them like a landscape scroll. Wrinkling his brow in wonder, he said, "That's part of the world outside, too, Senjumaru, but look at those wonderful halls and towers! They're just as grand-looking as the Hall of the Healing Buddha and the Great Lecture Hall here, don't you think? What do you suppose those buildings are?"

"There's a palace there where the emperor of all Japan lives. It's the grandest, noblest place in the whole outside world. But for some-one to live there, to be born as a Ruler with the Ten Virtues, he'd have to pile up an awful lot of merit in his former lives. That's why we have to practice so hard on the mountain here and let the roots of goodness grow deep down inside us."

Senjumaru did his best to encourage the younger child. But neither the encourager nor the encouraged found his curiosity to be easily or fully satisfied by this kind of exchange. According to their Master, the world outside was nothing but delusion. The scenes they viewed from the mountaintop, though they might seem lovely, were like moonlight reflected on the surface of the water, mere shadows, or foam on the sea. "Look at the clouds above the mountaintop," their Master would say. "Seen from afar, they seem as pure as snow, as bright as silver; but if you were in the midst of them, you'd find they weren't snow or silver but just dense mist. You boys know what it's like to be wrapped in the clouds of mist that rise from the valleys here on the mountain, don't you? The world outside is just like those clouds."

The boys felt almost convinced by their Master's helpful explanations, but not quite. Their greatest source of unease was the fact of never having actually seen the creature they called "a woman"— some sort of human being that lived in the outside world and was held to be the source of almost every calamity.

"They say I was only three when I came to the mountain, but you were out in the world until you were four, weren't you? So you must be able to remember something about it. Never mind about other women —you can remember something about your own mother, can't you?"

"Sometimes I try to remember how she looked, and I'm almost at the point of being able to, but then a kind of curtain seems to come between us. It's so frustrating! I just have some vague impressions of the way her warm breasts felt against my tongue, and the sweet smell of her milk. Women have these soft, full, rounded breasts, completely different from anything on a man's body—that much I do know. Memories of those things keep coming back, but the rest is vague, remote, like things that happened in a former life. . . ."

At night, the two boys had whispered conversations like these as they lay side by side in the room next to their Master's.

"If women are supposed to be devils, why should they have such soft breasts?" wondered Rurikōmaru.

"You're right. . . . How could a devil have nice, soft things like that?" echoed Senjumaru, bending his head a little to one side, as if starting to doubt his own memories.

Both of them should have been well aware from the sutras they'd been studying since early childhood what ferocious creatures women were, but they were quite unable to imagine what form their ferocity took. There were the lines from the *Sutra of King Udayana*: "Women are the worst workers of evil. They bind men and lead them through the gates of sin." And in the *Treatise on the Great Perfection of Wisdom Sutra*: "One can take up a sword against an enemy and conquer him, but much harder yet is it to prevent the tribe of women from harming one." So, then, women must be like robbers who bind men's hands behind their backs and drag them off to some sinister place. Then again there was the passage in the *Nirvana Sutra*: "Woman is the Great Demon King, capable of devouring men in their entirety." So perhaps women were monstrous beasts, larger and more fearsome than lions or tigers. And if the words of the *Great Treasure Store of Sutras* were true, where it says "One glance at a woman can mean the loss of all innocence in the eye. Better to look at a great serpent than on a woman," then the latter must be some kind of reptile that spits out poison from its body, like the huge pythons that lived in the depths of the mountains. Senjumaru and Rurikōmaru sought out fresh passages concerning women from many different sutras, then compared notes and exchanged opinions.

"You and I had two of these 'evil women' for mothers—they even cradled us on their laps! Yet we managed to come through it all right. So maybe women *aren't* like wild beasts and huge snakes that swallow people whole and spit out poison, after all."

"It says in the *Treatise on Consciousness Only*: 'Women are messengers from Hell'; so they must be even more terrifying than wild beasts and snakes to look at. We were very lucky not to have been killed by them!"

"But do you know the rest of that passage?" interrupted Senjumaru. "'Women are messengers from Hell, in whom the seeds of the

Buddha have long since been destroyed. Their outward appearance is like unto a bodhisattva, but their inner nature is like unto a demon.' Well, then, even if inside they're demons, they must have beautiful faces! The proof is that a merchant who came to worship here the other day was staring at me in a kind of trance and muttered to himself that some of these acolytes were as pretty as any girl."

"Me too! There've been lots of times when the older monks teased me for looking 'just like a girl.' I thought they meant I looked like a devil and got so upset I started crying once. But then someone said I shouldn't cry, they just meant I had a bodhisattva's face. I'm still not sure if I was being praised or blamed."

The more they talked to each other like this, the less they could grasp what sort of being a woman really was. Even on the holy mountain, sacred as it was to the memory of the founder, Dengyō Daishi, there were poisonous snakes and powerful wild animals. It was just like the world outside in that when spring came, the bush warblers sang and flowers bloomed, while in winter the trees and grasses withered and snow fell. The only difference was that there was not a single woman anywhere. But if the Buddha disliked women so much, how could they look like bodhisattvas? And why were women more dangerous than great serpents if their faces were so beautiful?

"If the world outside is an illusion, then women must be beautiful illusions too. And because they're illusions, ordinary, unenlightened men are led astray, like travelers in deep mountain country who get lost in the mists." Having thought about the matter carefully, the two boys came to this conclusion. A beautiful illusion, a beautiful nothing, that's what a woman was. This was the only conclusion that could satisfy them and calm their minds.

Now the younger Rurikōmaru's curiosity was a passing, whimsical thing, like the fancies of a young child about some fairyland. But something much stronger than mere curiosity lay coiled in his older friend's breast. Night after night Senjumaru gazed at the innocent face of the boy lying fast asleep across from him and wondered why he alone had to undergo such torments. He couldn't help envying the other his innocence. And when he did manage to close his eyes, images of women of every kind floated before him so vividly that his whole night's sleep was disturbed. At times they appeared as buddhas with the thirty-two signs of sanctity and seemed to embrace him in a purple-golden radiance; at others, they took the form of demons from the Aviçi Hell about to burn him up with tongues of flame that blazed from the tips of their eighteen horns. Sometimes, covered in a cold sweat, he would be wakened from his nightmares by Rurikō-maru, and would start up from his bed in terror.

"You were moaning and saying strange things in your sleep! Were you being attacked by some evil spirit?"

When Rurikōmaru asked him this, Senjumaru would bow his head in distress and say, his voice shaking a little, "I was being attacked by women in my dreams."

As the days passed, the look on Senjumaru's face, his gestures and movements, gradually lost any trace of a child's natural liveliness and simplicity. Whenever he had the chance of doing so unobserved by Rurikōmaru, he would stand in the inner sanctuary of the Great Lecture Hall and gaze dreamily at the lovely faces of the bodhisattvas Kannon and Miroku, lost in his own thoughts.

At such times the line from the *Treatise on Consciousness Only*, "Their outward appearance is like unto a bodhisattva," would fill his mind. Even if their inner selves were fiendish, even if their appearance was unreal, if there lived in the world human beings like the bodhisattvas worshiped in the many halls and pagodas of the holy mountain, what a grave sort of beauty they must possess! As he thought of this, he found his fear of women fading; all that remained was a strange kind of longing. He spent his days dreamily wandering among the sacred halls—the Hall of the Healing Buddha, the Lotus Hall, the Chapel of the Ordination Platform, the Chapel of the Mountain King —gazing at the holy images, the central ones with their attendant statues, and the host of carved angels that flew along the beams. He no longer indulged in speculation about women with his younger friend. The word "woman" came to Rurikōmaru's lips as easily as before, but now, for him, such talk had come to seem strange, and deeply sinful.

"Why can't I treat the whole business of women innocently, like Rurikōmaru? Why do evil fantasies of women come to mind even when I worship the sacred images of the buddhas there in front of me?"

Perhaps *this* was what was meant by "worldly passions". . . . The very thought made his skin crawl. He had been relying on the Master's assurance that there were no seeds of passion to be found on the holy mountain, yet had he himself not become a prisoner of the passions? All the more reason, then, to reveal his troubles to the Master. But a voice whispered over and over in his ear, "Do not reveal yourself so easily!" His troubles were painful, but at the same time sweet. He wanted to keep them all to himself, somehow.

It happened in the spring of the year that Senjumaru turned sixteen, and Rurikōmaru fourteen. The mountain cherries were in full bloom in the five valleys that surrounded the Eastern Precinct, and among the young green leaves that enfolded the forty-six hermitages, the sounds of the monastery bells were muffled by an atmosphere that was somehow heavy and oppressive. One day at dawn the two boys were on their way back from an errand they'd been sent on by their Master, to the high priest of Yokawa. They had stopped to rest a while, sitting in the shade of a cryptomeria in a place where passersby were few. Senjumaru let out a great sigh from time to time, gazing intently at the morning mist as it rose from the bottom of Paradise Valley and flowed up to join the clouds above the mountaintop.

"You must think I've been strange lately," he said suddenly, turning an unsmiling face toward his young friend. "Ever since we talked about the world outside, I've been worried about this matter of women; I think about it all the time. I don't want to actually meet a woman at all; but, to my shame, I find that when I kneel before the image of the Tathagata, no matter how hard I try to pray, images of women keep flitting before my eyes, with hardly a moment when I can concentrate on the Buddha. I'm disgusted with myself!"

Rurikōmaru was surprised to see tears flowing down Senjumaru's cheeks. It must be serious, he thought, if his friend was so distressed. Still, he couldn't understand how the problem of women could cause him so much pain.

"You won't be ordained for another year or two," continued Senjumaru, "but the Master said that I was to become a monk this year. But what's the point of taking a vow to follow the path to enlightenment in this shameful state of mind? Even if I practiced the six bodhisattva virtues and kept the five major precepts, this obsession of mine would ensure that I was never released from the round of birth and rebirth, to the end of time. Women may be just a sort of mirage, like a rainbow in the empty sky. But fools like me have to go right into the clouds to see for themselves that the rainbow is unreal, they won't learn just from listening to well-meaning advice. And that's why I've decided to slip away from the mountain just once before my ordination, and see for myself what this creature they call woman is really like. Only in that way can I hope to understand the nature of the illusion. And then the obsession will vanish—in a flash—I'm sure of it!"

"But won't the Master be very angry with you?"

Senjumaru's determination to go and discover the real nature of women so as to dispel the clouds of delusion in his mind touched Rurikōmaru deeply. He felt uneasy, though, at letting his only friend face the perils of the outside world alone. What would he do if he encountered the dragon god of Lake Biwa or the giant centipede of Mt. Mikami? Would he not perhaps be bound hand and foot by some woman and dragged into a dark cellar somewhere? And if by chance he should return alive, would he be allowed to stay on the holy mountain, after breaking the Master's strict rule never to leave the mountain without his permission?

Senjumaru's answer to all this was clear and firm: "Of course I realize that there are all sorts of dangers waiting for me outside here. But to be caught on the fangs of some wild animal or the blade of a bandit would also be a way of following the Law. Wouldn't it be better to lose my life than to continue being tormented by these passions? Besides, from what the older monks say, it seems the capital is only a journey of two leagues from here, so if I leave early in the morning, I might be back by a little past noon. And if the capital seems too far, I can just go to Sakamoto at the foot of the mountain. They say you can see women there too. If I can get away for just half a day without the Master noticing, I should be able to see my plan through. And even if I'm found out later, I'm sure the Master will be pleased to learn that these obstacles on the path of my enlightenment have been removed. I appreciate your worrying about me, but please don't try to stop me. My mind is made up."

Senjumaru looked at the disc of the sun as it rose, gliding through the dawn mists that hung over the surface of Lake Biwa, spread out beneath them. Laying a hand on Rurikōmaru's shoulder, he said to him soothingly: "And today is the perfect chance for it. If I leave now, I can be back by two or so. I'll return safe and sound, you just wait and see, with some interesting tales to tell you this evening."

"If you really are going, then take me along with you," said Ru-rikōmaru, weeping. "With luck, you should come back safely, but even if it is only a half day's journey, something might happen to you. Who knows when we might meet again? You say you're ready to give your life if you have to: how can I say goodbye to you like this, it's too unkind! And what if the Master asked me where you went—what could I answer? If I'm going to be scolded anyway, I'd rather leave the mountain with you. If it's 'following the Law' for you, why then, it's the same for me as well!"

"No. *My* mind is chained in darkness, yours isn't. We're as different as charcoal and snow. You're as pure as crystal; there's no need for you to test your faith in ways that put you in danger. If something happened to you, what excuse could I ever offer to our Master? If it were some amusing place I was going to, I'd never leave you behind, but the outside world is a disgusting, terrifying sort of place. If all goes well and I come back, the scales will have fallen from my eyes and I'll be able to tell you all about it, in detail, so you'll understand the meaning of illusion without having to see the outside world yourself. Just stay here and wait. If the Master asks anything, say you wandered off on a mountain path and lost sight of me."

Senjumaru drew closer to Rurikōmaru and pressed his cheek sadly against the younger boy's, remaining like that for some time. To leave behind—even for a short while—the holy mountain and this friend from whom he'd never been parted was both a painful and a daring thing to do. He felt something akin to the excitement of a warrior going into battle for the first time. The fear that he might actually die and the hope that he could win through and return victorious swirled within him.

Two, then three days passed, but Senjumaru did not return. Fear-ing that he might have tumbled into one of the mountain gorges and died there, his fellow acolytes and monks split up into several parties and set out in all directions, scouring the mountain for traces of him, but in vain.

"Master, I've done a very wicked thing: I lied to you the other day." Rurikōmaru prostrated himself before the Master and confessed how for the very first time he'd broken the commandment against false speech. It was about ten days after Senjumaru had disappeared. "I was lying when I said I lost sight of Senjumaru on the way back from Yokawa. He isn't anywhere on the mountain now. I know it was wrong of me to tell an outright lie, even if someone asked me to. Please forgive me. Oh, why didn't I stop Senjumaru from ever leaving?" The boy lay flat on the floor, his body shaking with sobs of remorse.

He had looked on Senjumaru as his elder brother and now where was he? Was he sleeping among the tufts of moor grass somewhere, wet with dew? He'd firmly promised to come back within half a day, so something *must* have happened to him. Knowing this, it made no sense to be searching the mountain when they ought to be combing the world outside instead. And if he had fortunately survived, Rurikō-maru hoped they'd save him from that fearful world without delay. These were his feelings as he decided to risk a harsh scolding and tell the Master everything about Senjumaru's motives for leaving the mountain.

"Well, it's like tossing a pebble into the ocean. There's no telling what might have become of him, out there in the world." The Master had closed his eyes and taken a deep breath before speaking slowly, with great concentration, so as to impress the gravity of the situation on the lad. "Still, you did well not to be misled yourself and to stay on the mountain. You're the younger of the two, but your character has always been different from Senjumaru's. It's a matter of breeding, I suppose."

Senjumaru's parents, though well-to-do, came from peasant stock, while Rurikōmaru was the scion of an aristocratic family that served at court. The word "breeding" had often been used when people drew comparisons between the two boys, in looks or temperament. Rurikōmaru had heard it himself before, but now for the first time from the Master's own lips.

"It was wicked of him to break the rules and decide on his own to go, but I daresay he's paying for his foolishness now, so I feel sorry for him too. He may have been eaten by wild dogs or attacked by bandits—I'm sure something bad has happened to him. Perhaps we should assume he's no longer of this world and offer up prayers for his soul. You, at any rate, must be careful never to give way to worldly passions. Let Senjumaru's fate be a lesson to you!" The Master looked into Rurikōmaru's large, lively eyes and gently patted him on the back, as if to say "What a good, clever lad you are!"

From then on, each night Rurikōmaru had to sleep alone in the room right next to the Master's. "I'll be back soon," Senjumaru had said when they parted, and then went off toward Yase along a rugged, almost untraveled mountain path, so as not to be seen by anyone. Night after night in his dreams Rurikōmaru saw that receding figure growing smaller and smaller, vanishing in the distance. Looking back, he felt a certain guilt at not having forced Senjumaru to give up his plan, so likely to lead to his death. Yet, had he gone with him then, what disaster might have awaited him? The thought made him bless his own good fortune. "The Buddha was protecting me. From now on I'm going to do whatever my Master says, so as to become in the end as pure in heart as any holy man should be. Then I'll pray constantly for Senjumaru's salvation."

Rurikōmaru vowed this repeatedly to himself. If he really did have the sort of gifts the Master was always praising him for, then he would surely be able to endure every sort of hard and painful practice, finally awakening to the truth of the Dharma Realm of Suchness and attaining the state of Wondrous Enlightenment. The very thought made the flame of faith blaze up within his earnest young mind.

At last autumn came. A half year had passed since Senjumaru had left the mountain. The loud whirring of cicadas which had filled the mountainsides was now replaced by the melancholy sound of the *higurashi* or "evening cicada," and the leaves of the forest trees grew gradually yellower. One evening after vespers Rurikōmaru was descending the stone stairway in front of the Monju Pavilion, going toward his quarters, when he heard someone calling to him from the top of the stairway in a low, hesitant voice: "Excuse me, but might you be Rurikōmaru? I've come with a message for you from my master, from the village of Fukakusa in Yamashiro. I was told to hand this letter to you directly." The man, half-hidden in the shadows of the pavilion gate, beckoned to him, making many little bows and revealing in a meaningful fashion the edge of a letter which he had concealed in his kimono sleeve. "Don't worry, it's all explained here. My master told me to show you this letter, in private if possible, and bring back your reply."

Rurikōmaru looked suspiciously at the fellow, a man of about twenty with scraggly whiskers and the lowly manner of a servant. He took the letter, though, and looked at the writing on the front. "Why, it's Senjumaru's hand!" he cried out despite himself. The man, trying to quiet him, went on to say: "Yes, it's true. It's good you haven't forgotten. The sender of this letter is indeed Senjumaru, your good friend and now my master. This past spring, soon after leaving the mountain, he fell into the clutches of a slave-trader, and had a very hard time. But his luck hadn't run out, for just two months ago he was sold to be the servant of a rich man in Fukakusa. His gentle looks won the heart of the rich man's daughter, and now he's the son-in-law of the family, with everything he could desire.

"And so I've brought you this letter which will tell you all about the world outside, just as my master promised. It's not at all the terrifying place he thought it was when he was on the holy mountain. Women aren't like snakes or wild animals at all. No, they're prettier than the flowers of spring and as loving as the Buddha. It's all explained in detail in this letter.

"My master Senjumaru is loved by a lot of other women too, not only that rich man's daughter. Tomorrow, it's off to Kamizaki; today, to Kanishima and Eguchi—he wanders about here and there, attended by a crowd of courtesans more beautiful even than the twenty-five bodhisattvas. He passes his days in pleasure, like a butterfly in springtime, fluttering over the fields and hills. And here you are, knowing nothing about what the world out there has to offer, leading a dreary life on this mountain. My master feels sorry for you; he wants you to come to Fukakusa, if possible, and share his happiness, for old times' sake. I can see for myself that you're an even better-looking and more charming young acolyte than my master must have been. It's a terrible waste for you to spend your life up here. Just think how admired and wanted someone with your looks would be if you went out into the world! Anyway, please read this letter and see whether or not I'm telling the truth. And then by all means come with me to Fukakusa. I have to leave now for Katata Bay in the province of Ōmi, but I'll be back here by dawn tomorrow. Think it over carefully till then; and when you've decided, wait for me beneath this gate, taking care that no one sees you. I promise that nothing bad will come of this. And nothing would make my master happier than to see you return with me!"

Looking at the man's smiling face, Rurikōmaru felt somehow afraid. He hadn't had time fully to taste the joy of this unexpected message from the friend he'd not seen for six months; and now this grave proposition, which might well determine the rest of his life, was suddenly thrust before him. It seemed for a while as if he couldn't breathe, as if his eyes had grown dim. He stood there trembling, rooted to the spot.

> *I don't know where to begin or where to stop, trying to describe all that's happened to me since that day,* the letter began. *I'd have liked to go to the holy mountain myself so I could see you again after so long and tell you everything in person. But for one who has broken the monastic rules, the lofty summit of the One Vehicle of Salvation towers too high above me to look upon; and the valley of the One Taste of Truth lies too deep for me to approach. . . .*

Rurikōmaru stood there blankly, hardly knowing what he was doing. He held the letter loosely in one hand, hurriedly reading a sentence here, a sentence there.

> *During all the time that has passed since I left, promising to return within half a day, you must have thought I'd deceived you. That thought fills me with pain and regret. I never had any such intention. I was on my way back that evening and had already reached Kiraragoe when suddenly a man rushed out at me from the shadows. I found myself being gagged and blindfolded and dragged who knows where. Horrified, I thought that the Buddha's punishment had been swift indeed, that I'd be taken alive across the River of the Dead to experience the eight torments of Hell!*

But though there were praiseworthy lines like those above, there was also one beginning boldly with the words "It's a sheer delight!" which seemed to hold neither gods nor buddhas in awe.

The truth is, the outside world is not *a dream,* not *an illusion. It's a sheer delight—in fact a paradise, the Western Pure Land here on earth. I have no use any more for the doctrine of "Three Thousand Phenomena in a Single Thought" or for the meditation on "The Perfect Interpenetration of the Three Truths." Believe me, the joy of being just a common layman involved with the passions is infinitely preferable to being an ascetic practicing the "Perfect and Sudden Way" to enlightenmment. I urge you to change your way of thinking and come down from the mountain at once.*

Could this really be Senjumaru speaking? Senjumaru, who had been so devout, who had hated the very sound of the word "passion"—could these really be his thoughts? The sacrilegious comments that filled the letter, the strangely excited tone, the enthusiasm which seemed somehow overwrought, all aroused a feeling of revulsion in Rurikōmaru, yet at the same time, and to an equal degree, caused the curiosity about the outside world that had been building up inside him for a long time to well forth.

Tomorrow morning will do very well, so please think it over carefully. It goes without saying that you mustn't speak of this to anyone. Everything the monks on that mountain tell you is a pack of lies. They'll say anything to an innocent lad like you to make you give up any thought of the greater world outside. Anyway, take a good look at this letter and then decide for yourself. All right?

The servant could see from the look on Rurikōmaru's face that he was hesitant and suspicious, so he spoke to him again in a reassuring manner, then, with several hurried little bows, ran down the steps.

Even so, Rurikōmaru could not stop trembling. The man had left behind a burden so heavy it overwhelmed the heart of this innocent, serious-minded youth. His whole future would depend on the reply he had to give by the next morning. This was the first time he had ever had to make such a great decision for himself. That realization itself made his heart pound uncontrollably.

That night, overcome by anxiety and excitement, he was incapable of calmly considering the problem he'd been presented with. He decided to wait until he was feeling calmer and then try again to read that strange letter filled with the most amazing revelations about the long-hidden secret of "women." Leaving it sitting on top of his desk, he closed his eyes and earnestly prayed to the Buddha. The letter brought news of his beloved friend, yet it made him feel angry and resentful since it amounted to a surprise attack on his firm determination to devote himself to the most intense religious training and to accrue merit in accordance with the karmic relations he had established.

"If I read it again, it will lead me astray. Wouldn't it be better to burn it?" he told himself; but the next minute he laughed at his own cowardice: "I'm not such a weakling that I need to be so afraid!" Whether he was to be led astray or not depended solely on the will of the Buddha. Senjumaru claimed that the world outside was not an illusion, but how far was he to be believed? How much of it was mere temptation? And if he couldn't resist that kind of temptation, hadn't he already been abandoned by the Buddha? A sneaking curiosity that kept raising its head left him unable to resist asking such questions and making such excuses.

> It is hard to convey the gentleness and beauty of women, either in words or pictures. To what shall I compare them?... Just yesterday I embarked at Yodo harbor and went to a place called Eguchi where from the houses along the riverbank came a throng of courtesans paddling their little boats toward us. It seemed like Seishi Bodhisattva's descent from Paradise, or an apparition of

the Willow Kannon: I was filled with joy and gratitude! Before long they surrounded our boat and began singing popular songs so gaily that I begged them to sing one for me—any one would do. Then one of the women, beating time on the gunwale of the boat, sang: "Even holy Shakamuni / Who went from passion to perfect peace / Once knew the mother of his son / Ragora, 'tis said." Over and over she sang it, so entertainingly....

Throughout this passage Senjumaru seemed to be doing his utmost to destroy Rurikōmaru's devotion to the Way. It was a shout of joy and praise, from a youth who for the first time in his sixteen years of life had been shown what the world could be. In one part of the letter, Senjumaru became ecstatic; in another, he railed against the Master who had deceived him for so long; in another, he vowed eternal friendship for Rurikōmaru, his childhood companion, and urged him to leave the mountain. Rurikōmaru felt he had never been so impressed by anything he'd ever read before, not even the words of sacred scripture.

The Pure Land of Perfect Bliss, believed to be billions of worlds away, lies just below your mountain, and living bodhisattvas in great numbers are waiting to welcome you there at any time.

What reason was there for continuing to doubt this amazing fact? Senjumaru hadn't actually mentioned them, but there must be kalavinka birds and parrots and peacocks filling the air with their cries. There would be pavilions made of mother-of-pearl and agate, stairways of gold and silver and garnet. A wondrous world of fantasy abruptly rose before Rurikōmaru's eyes, as in a fairy tale. Why should it be an obstacle to enlightenment, to spend a while in such a pleasant world? Why should the Master have such contempt for it, and try to keep them all away from it? He wanted to know the reason he had to overcome this "temptation," if he was to try to overcome it.

He spread the letter out in the dim lamplight and read it over and over again. That whole night he spent in thought, without a moment's sleep. He struggled to find some means of denying the facts in the letter, taxing his knowledge and powers of understanding to their limits. He tried listening to the voice of conscience and seeking guidance from the Buddha, to a degree that anyone would find commendable. In the end, there was nothing to keep him from taking the final step apart from his attachment to his accustomed life in the monastery and his blind faith in the precepts of his Master. But those two things had an unexpectedly strong hold on his mind. If he were to fight off the desire to leave the mountain, he would have to strengthen those two feelings to the utmost.

"So, am I willing to believe Senjumaru and deny the teachings of the Buddha, the precepts of my Master? To go so far as to call the Buddha and my Master liars? Do I honestly think that will be the end of it?" he muttered aloud. The fleeting world outside must surely be a pleasant place, as Senjumaru said. But would it do to cast aside in one morning the firm faith he had built up over fourteen years for the sake of such diversions? Had he not recently made a vow to endure the harshest, most painful ascetic practice? Even if he could have worldly pleasures in the present life, wouldn't he have to endure pains ten or twenty times as great if, incurring the Buddha's displeasure, he fell into the fires of Hell in the next life?

The word "breeding" suddenly came to mind. He and Senjumaru had had different characters since earliest childhood. He *knew* the Buddha was protecting him. It was that, surely, that had made him think of retribution in the next life just now. So long as there was a next life, how could he fail to fear the prospect of punishment? It was because there was hope of a life to come that the Master had forbidden them the pleasures of this life. Senjumaru, it seemed, did not believe; but *he* would—he would believe in the next life, and in perdition. That itself would demonstrate the superiority of his character. When the Master praised him, wasn't he referring precisely to that?

These thoughts descended on Rurikōmaru like a revelation from Heaven. At first it was like lightning flashing, then as if the waves of the sea were gradually spreading, washing over his soul, filling his body to overflowing. He felt refreshed, like someone moved by the clear sounds of music; it seemed to him the sort of heightened religious emotion that only an ascetic who has entered the realm of *samadhi* could experience. Rurikōmaru found himself folding his hands in prayer to the unseen Buddha and saying in his heart again and again: "Forgive me, please, for being foolish enough to give in to the temptations of this life even for a little while, and being willing to throw away the rewards of the world to come. I promise never again to allow those wicked thoughts to arise the way I did tonight, so please forgive me."

No, no matter what, he would not be misled by anyone. If Senjumaru wanted to indulge in wordly pleasures, let him do so on his own. And then let him fall headfirst into the Aviçi Hell in the next life, and suffer there for endless aeons. And Rurikōmaru, meanwhile, would travel to the Western Pure Land and gaze down from on high on Senjumaru crying in torment. His faith was now unshakable, regardless of what anyone said. He had stopped himself in the nick of time; but now he was safe, now there was nothing to worry about.

As Rurikōmaru arrived at this resolution, the long autumn night grew gradually lighter, and the clear sound of the bell calling them to early matins was heard. With a mind many times more tense than usual, he respectfully presented himself in the chamber of his Master, who seemed only just to have awakened.

Now the man sent by Senjumaru had been waiting beside the stone steps leading to the Monju Pavilion from before dawn. But though Rurikōmaru did meet him there, the boy's reply was an unexpected one: "For reasons of my own, I've decided not to leave the holy mountain, despite the attractions of life elsewhere. I'd rather have the blessing of the Buddha than the love of women." He drew the letter from the night before out of the folds of his kimono, and went on: "Tell your master that I hope to gain peace in the next life, even if I have to suffer in this one. . . . And this letter will disturb my peace of mind, so please take it back with you."

The man blinked his eyes in amazement and seemed about to say something, when Rurikōmaru hurriedly threw the letter onto the ground and set off toward the monastery without so much as a backward look.

And so winter came on. "You'll be fifteen next year, and when I think of what happened to Senjumaru, it seems best for you to take your full vows as soon as possible, in the spring," said the Master.

However, Rurikōmaru's mind *had* been disturbed by the letter from his old friend, and he wasn't able to maintain his serenity for very long—he had merely repressed his feelings in a burst of religious fervor. Gradually he too began to share the obsessions that had so troubled Senjumaru. The time came when, like his friend, he too would see the forms of women in his dreams, and feel bewitched by the images of the bodhisattvas in the chapels and pagodas. He even began to wish he hadn't returned Senjumaru's letter that day. There were days when he became aware of himself waiting for the messenger from Fukakusa to come again. He was afraid to let the Master see his face.

Nonetheless, he still had faith in the divine protection of the Buddha, and he was not about to act as rashly as Senjumaru had. So one day he presented himself reverently before the Master and confessed:

"Master, have pity on me—forgive me my folly. I can't laugh at Senju-maru's action any more. Teach me the way to put out the flames of passion and make my fantasies of women disappear. I will endure even the harshest rites to be free of them."

"It took courage for you to confess this to me," said the Master. "Your intentions are admirable. You're a fine young acolyte, I assure you. Whenever those evil thoughts begin to arise, you must seek the Buddha's compassion through wholehearted prayer. For the next twenty-one days, you are to purify your body with cold water each day without fail and seclude yourself in the Lotus Hall. Your reward will then surely come, and these shameful visions will cease." Such were the Master's instructions.

It was the night of the twenty-first day, the end of Rurikōmaru's special devotions. Fatigued from those long days of ascetic practice, he was leaning against a pillar in the Lotus Hall, dozing, when the figure of a noble-looking old man appeared in a dream. He seemed to be calling Rurikōmaru's name repeatedly. "I have good news for you," he told him. "In a former life, you were an official at the court of a certain Indian king. At that time, there was a beautiful woman in the capital who was very much in love with you. However, since you were already a person with his mind set firmly on the Way and not given to worldly lusts, she was unable to lead you astray. It was due to your merit in resisting that woman's charms that you had the good fortune in this life of being brought up under the guidance of your Master and receiving his invaluable instruction. The woman who loved you, though, has been unable to forget you and is now living on this mountain in a different form. As retribution for her sin in having tried to win you over, she was reborn as a bird; but having spent her life in this holy place where she hears the words of the sutras chanted every morning and evening, she will gain rebirth next time in the Western Pure Land. In the end, seated together with you on

one of the lotuses that bloom in Paradise, she will appear as a bodhisattva, bathed in the radiance of the buddhas of all ten directions.

"The woman is now lying alone, badly wounded and near death
on the summit of Mt. Shakagatake. Knowing you are troubled by
dreams of women, I urge you to go to her at once. Then she can
enter Amida Buddha's Pure Land ahead of you and from there help
you in your quest for enlightenment. Your present distractions should
vanish without a trace. . . . It was out of admiration for your strong
faith that I came down from the Tushita Heaven, as a messenger of
Fugen Bodhisattva. So that your faith may not falter, I give you this
crystal rosary. You must never doubt my words!"

When Rurikōmaru returned to full consciousness, the old man was
nowhere to be seen; but there was indeed a crystal rosary laid upon
his lap, where it shone as brightly as beads of dew at dawn.

Trying to climb to the top of Shakagatake in a piercingly cold wind
early in the morning of a day close to the end of December must
have been, to the young acolyte, a task harder than the twenty-one
days of purification with cold water. Yet Rurikōmaru felt neither pain
nor hindrance as he climbed the steep mountain path, so eager was
he to see in her present form the woman with whom he seemed to
have such deep links, extending over past, present, and future lives.
Even the snow, white and fluffy as cotton, that began to fall as he
climbed served as fuel to make the flames of his single-minded
fervor burn all the brighter. On he went, stumbling occasionally, through
a landscape where everything—sky and earth, valleys and wood-
lands—was gradually enfolded in a sheet of silver.

At last it seemed that he had reached the summit. The snow fell in
gentle eddies and covered the ground, and in its midst there was
something whiter yet, something that seemed like the very spirit of
the snow itself—a bird of unknown type with a painful-looking
wound beneath one wing, flopping about in the snow, crying out in

pain as drops of blood fell here and there like scattered scarlet petals. Catching sight of this, Rurikōmaru ran forward and held her closely in his arms, like a mother-bird sheltering her chick beneath her wings. Then, from the depths of the snowstorm which seemed to smother all sounds, he raised his voice and chanted loudly, and still more loudly, the saving name of Amida. The crystal beads that he was holding in his hand he placed about her neck.

He wondered if he might not die of cold before she did of her wound. Pressing his face down against her, he covered her body with his own; and onto his hair, arranged in the charming and quite elaborate style of the temple acolyte, there fell softly, steadily, something white—bird's feathers, perhaps, or powdery snow.

The Gourmet Club

TRANSLATED BY
Paul McCarthy

I daresay the members of the Gourmet Club loved the pleasures of the table not a whit less than they loved those of the bedroom. They were a collection of idlers with no occupations apart from gambling, buying women, and eating fine food. Whenever they discovered some novel flavor, they took as much pride and pleasure in it as if they'd found a beautiful woman for themselves. If they found a cook able to produce such flavors, a genius of a cook, they might employ him in their homes at wages equal to what they would spend to monopolize the favors of a first-class geisha. It was their conviction that "if there were genius in the arts, then of course there must be genius in cookery as well." For in their view, cooking *was* an art, capable of yielding artistic effects that—at least so far as they were concerned—put poetry, music, and painting in the shade. Not only after a splendid meal, but even at the moment they all gathered around a table piled high with delicious things, they felt the same kind of excitement, the same rapture one does on hearing the finest orchestral music. It took them to such giddy heights that it seemed only natural they should think that these epicurean pleasures were as much of the spirit as of the flesh. But the devil, it seems, is as powerful as God, for when any of the sensual pleasures (and not only those of the table) are taken to their furthest point, there is a danger of losing oneself entirely in them. . . .

Thus, as a result of their gormandizing, each and every one of them was afflicted year-round with a large pot-belly. And it was not only their bellies, of course: their bodies brimmed with excess fat; their cheeks and thighs were as plump and oily as the pig's flesh used in making pork belly cooked in soy sauce. Three of them were diabetics, and almost all the club members suffered from gastric dilatation. Some had come close to dying from appendicitis. Still, in part from petty vanity and partly out of strict fidelity to the epicure-anism to which they were so devoted, none of them was worried about illness. Or, if perhaps one of them did feel some inward fear, nobody was so craven as to quit the club on that account.

"We'll all be dead of stomach cancer one of these days," they used to tell each other, laughing. They were rather like ducks that are kept in darkness and stuffed with rich food so that their flesh will become tender and succulent. The point at which their bellies became ab-solutely crammed with food would presumably be when their lives came to an end. Until then, they would live on, never knowing when to stop eating, with belches continually erupting from their heavy-laden stomachs.

There were only five members of this society of eccentrics. When-ever they were free—and since they were unemployed, this meant virtually every day—they would gather at someone's house or on the second floor of some club and spend their afternoons mostly in gam-bling. From traditional Japanese card games like boar-deer-butterfly to bridge, napoleon, poker, twenty-one, and five hundred, they played an endless variety of betting games, at which they were all equally adept, good players to a man. Then when night came, the money they'd won would be pooled and used to finance that evening's feast. Sometimes it would be held at a member's house and some-times at a restaurant in town. But they soon grew tired of the famous restaurants in central Tokyo: the Mikawaya in Akasaka, the Kinsui in

Hamachō, the Okitsu in Azabu, the Jishōken in Tabata, the Shima-mura, Ōtokiwa, Kotokiwa, Hasshin and Naniwaya in Nihombashi—they'd eaten their way through all of these fine Japanese-style restaurants any number of times and no longer had any interest in them. "What'll we eat tonight?" was their sole matter of concern from the moment they opened their eyes in the morning. And even as they gambled away the afternoon, they were all thinking about the evening's menu.

"I want my fill of some good soft-shelled turtle soup tonight," someone would moan during a lull in the card game, and immediately fierce gluttony would run like electricity through the little group, none of whom had yet been able to come up with a good idea for that night. All would agree to this at once, with the greatest enthusiasm, and their eyes and faces took on a curious shine which hadn't been there when they were merely playing cards—a wild, degraded look, like that of the hungry ghosts of Buddhist lore.

"Turtle? Eat our fill of turtle soup? But I wonder if we can get really good turtle at a Tokyo restaurant...," another man would mutter anxiously to himself. This was mumbled so low as to be barely audible, yet it served to diminish the ardor of the company, which had flared up just a moment before. Even the way they played their cards lost something of its energy.

Then someone else might suddenly suggest: "You know, we'll never find it in Tokyo. I say we leave for Kyoto by the night train and go to the Maruya in Kamishichiken-machi. That way we can have turtle for lunch tomorrow!"

"Good idea! We'll go to Kyoto—or anywhere, for that matter! Once you've set your heart on eating something, you've just *got* to have it!"

Their relief was patently visible, and redoubled appetites were felt rumbling up from the pits of their stomachs. So, impelled by their desire for turtle, they endured being shaken about on the night train for Kyoto; and the next evening they headed back to Tokyo with ample bellies abrim with turtle soup, comfortably swaying to the motion of the return journey.

They grew more and more capricious, going off to Osaka to have sea bream and hot tea-over-rice, or to Shimonoseki for blowfish. Longing for the taste of Akita sandfish, they made expeditions to the snow-blown towns of the north country. And eventually their tongues lost all taste for the usual "fine cuisine"; lick and slurp as they might, they could no longer discover the excitement and joy in eating that they demanded. They were of course sick to death of Japanese food, and as for Western food, they knew they could never find the real thing unless they actually went abroad. There remained Chinese food— that rich cuisine said to be the most developed and varied in the world; but to them, even that had become as tasteless and boring as a glass of water.

Now, since they were the sort who'd worry more about satisfying their stomachs than about a gravely ill parent, it goes without saying that their anxiety and ill-humor had reached quite a pitch. They scoured all the eateries of Tokyo, hoping to impress their fellow members by discovering some wondrous new flavor. They were like curio collectors rummaging about in dubious secondhand shops on the off chance of making an unusual find. One of them tried some bean-jam cakes at a night stall somewhere on the Ginza and, proclaiming them the most delicious item to be found in present-day Tokyo, displayed his discovery to the other members with the greatest pride. Another bragged that a vendor who came every night around midnight to the geisha-house area in Karasumori sold the best Chinese dumplings in the world. But when the rest of the group, led on by such reports, actually tried these plebeian delights, they found that the discoverer's taste buds had usually been the victim of his over-heated imagination. To tell the truth, they *all* seemed to be getting a bit funny in the head lately, driven by their gluttony. Someone who laughed at another's discovery would himself get terrifically excited about some slightly unusual flavor he'd come across, regardless of whether it was good or bad.

"No matter what we eat, it's all the same—no improvement. It looks like we'll have to find ourselves a really first-class chef and create some completely new dishes."

"Find a chef of genius, or else offer prize money to anyone who can think up a really amazing dish."

"But we're not going to give prizes for bean-jam cakes or Chinese dumplings, no matter how good they might be. We need something rich and striking, suited to a big banquet."

"In other words, we need a kind of orchestral cuisine!"

This is the sort of conversation they held. I trust by now the reader will have formed a good idea of just what kind of group this Gourmet Club was, and what kind of situation the members found themselves in. I felt a preface of sorts was necessary before telling the story that fol-lows.

Count G. was the most moneyed and idlest member of the club; he was also the youngest, possessed of a sharp wit, a wild imagina-tion, and the sturdiest stomach of all. Since there were only five members in all, there was no need for a formal president, but the club's usual meeting place was on the upper floor of Count G.'s mansion, and since this served as their headquarters, the Count natu-rally became a kind of manager, occupying a position very like that of president. It goes without saying, then, that when it came to hunt-ing down some rare delicacy and feasting on it, he took twice as many pains, devoted twice as much nervous energy to the task as any of the other members. And they, of course, all placed their highest hopes of such discoveries on the Count, always the most creative of the group. If anyone was to win the prize money, surely it would be he. And if it meant his introducing them to some splendid new culinary achievement, and awakening their jaded taste buds to some blissful new experience, something subtle and profound, they would be only too happy to pay it. This, in their heart of hearts, was what they all ultimately wanted.

"A symphony of foods! An orchestral cuisine!"

These words kept coming to the Count's mind. Food whose flavors would make the flesh melt and raise the soul to heaven. Food like music that, once heard, would make men dance madly, dance themselves to death. Food one just had to eat, and the more one ate, the more the unbearably delicious flavors would entwine themselves around the tongue until at last one's stomach burst open. If only he could create such food, thought the Count, he would become a great artist. And even if he couldn't, all sorts of wild fantasies of food floated up and disappeared endlessly within the mind of this highly imaginative individual. Asleep or awake, he saw only dreams of food. . . .

Out of the darkness, he saw puffs of white steam rise temptingly. Something smelled awfully good. A smell like lightly scorched *mochi*. A smell like roasting duck. The smell of pork fat. The smell of leeks and garlic and onions. A smell like beef hotpot. Smells strong and fragrant and sweet, all mixed together, rising from the midst of the steam. Looking steadily into the darkness, he could see five or six objects hovering in the steam-filled air. One was a soft white block of something—pork fat? devil's-tongue?—that trembled in the air. With every movement a thick, honey-like liquid dripped, dripped, dripped onto the ground. Where it fell, it formed a brown-colored little mound with a syrupy sheen. . . .

To the left was the finest, largest shellfish—perhaps a kind of clam —that the Count had ever seen. The upper half shell kept opening and closing. Then, as it opened fully, he could see a strange mollusc, neither clam nor oyster, alive and wriggling inside. It was black and hard-looking toward the top, while the bottom was slimy white, phlegm-like. As he watched, odd-looking wrinkles began to appear on the surface of that viscous white substance. At first they were like the wrinkles on a dried plum; then gradually they got deeper, until finally the entire mollusc became hard, like a piece of paper that has been chewed on and spat out. Then from both sides of the thing small bubbles, like the ones that crabs emit, began to boil up; and soon the whole shellfish was covered with bubbles, welling up like cotton-balls erupting from their pods, and the mollusc itself vanished from sight. . . . *Ah yes, it's being boiled*, thought Count G. to himself. Just then there came to his nostrils a whiff of clam hotpot, or rather, something many times more delicious. One by one the bubbles began to burst and form a liquid that looked like melted soap. The liquid ran along the shell's edges and dripped onto the ground, giving off warm steam. In the shell itself, alongside the by now solidified mollusc, to left and right there suddenly appeared two round objects, like *mochi* cakes offered on an altar. They looked much softer than *mochi*, though, and quivered slightly, like fine-grained tofu submerged in water. . . . *Those must be the adductors*, the Count reflected. Then the objects gradually turned a brownish color and small cracks began to appear here and there on their surfaces.

Finally the various foods that were collected there began all at once to roll about. The ground on which they rested suddenly thrust itself up from below—it had gone unnoticed up to now because of its size, but what had seemed to be the ground was in fact a giant tongue, and all those foods were jumbled together in an immense mouth. Soon upper and lower rows of teeth began slowly to converge, like mountain ranges pushing up from the depths of the earth and downward from the sky. They started to crush the foods that rested on the tongue, and the mashed foods turned into a fluid like puss from an abscess, a kind of sludge upon the tongue's surface. The tongue licked the four walls of the oral cavity with relish, undulating like a stingray. From time to time, with a great spasm it would thrust the liquid mass down toward the throat. Still, there were small shreds of food that had been crushed into the spaces between the teeth or to the bottom of deep cracks that had eaten into their surfaces. These shreds were layered one on top of another, tangled and stuck together. Then a giant toothpick appeared and, having dug out the shreds of food one by one, deposited them on the tongue. The food that had just been swallowed came rushing back into the mouth in the form of a great belch. The tongue once again became slimy with fluid. Again and again the food was swallowed down, only to be brought back up with the inevitable belch. . . .

The Count awoke to the sound of burps erupting deep in his gullet: clearly, he'd had too much of that abalone soup at the Chinese restaurant this evening.

It happened one evening after some ten nights of dreams like the one just described. After yet another dull club dinner, the members were having a smoke, looks of boredom on their faces. Leaving them behind, the Count slipped out for a stroll. His aim, however, was not to help his digestion. No—he regarded the dreams he'd been having lately as a sort of oracle and was sure he was on the verge of making a breakthrough of some kind. He felt a premonition that it might happen this very night, in fact.

It was almost nine o'clock on a cold winter's night when the Count
fled the clubroom housed in his own mansion in the Surugadai section of the city. He wore an olive-colored fedora and a camel-hair
coat with a thick astrakhan collar. As he strolled along with his ivory-
knobbed ebony walking stick in hand, trying to hold back the usual
burps from within, he wended his way down the slope toward Imagawakōji. It was quite a busy thoroughfare, but needless to say the
Count didn't spare a glance at the fancy goods and sundries stores or
bookshops that lined the street, nor at the faces of the passersby or
their clothes. On the other hand, if he passed even the humblest little
eatery, let alone a more imposing place, his nose became as keen as
a starving dog's. As all Tokyoites probably know, if you go two or
three blocks down Imagawakōji from Surugadai, you come to the
No. 1 Chinese Restaurant on the right side of the street. Stopping in
front of it, the Count's nostrils began to twitch. (He possessed a very
keen nose and could generally judge the level of a restaurant's cuisine by a sniff or two.) After a moment, though, he started briskly
off in the direction of Kudan, swinging his stick, a look of resignation
on his face.

He had just cut through a narrow lane and was about to enter a
dark, lonely neighborhood near the moat when two Chinese men
with toothpicks in their mouths came toward him, brushing against
his shoulder as they passed. Since, as we have noted, the Count was
intent only on food and didn't even glance at any pedestrians, he
would normally have paid no attention to the two men; but at the
instant they passed, a whiff of *shao-hsing* rice wine reached his nostrils. He turned and glanced at the others' faces.

*Well now, these two fellows have just been eating Chinese food, so
maybe there's a new restaurant somewhere nearby,* thought the Count,
cocking his head to one side. Just then, the sound of a Chinese violin
being played somewhere far off came drifting to his ears—a sound

with overtones of sadness and yearning in the night's darkness.

The Count stood listening intently for a while there in the darkness
by the moat near Ushigafuchi Park. The sound came, not from from
Kudanzaka with its bright lights glittering in the distance, but from
deep in the back alleyways of one of the dead-quiet, unfrequented
neighborhoods toward Hitotsubashi. Yes, that was where it came
from, trembling in the freezing air of the winter night, a high-pitched,
intermittent sound, sharp as the creaking of a well sweep, thin as drawn
wire—echoing, as if about to die away. When at last that screechy
sound had reached its peak, it suddenly stopped, like a burst bal-
loon, and immediately there was the sound of clapping—there must
have been an audience of ten at least. The sudden applause came
from closer by than he'd expected.

They're having a banquet, and it's Chinese food. But where can it be?

The applause continued for some time. It would die down, and then
someone would start to clap again, and in response the applause
burst forth again, with a sound like the flapping of pigeons' wings. It
came like the swell of waves, retreating and then surging forward
against the shore. And, like a bird twittering, half-choked by the sea
spray, from among the oncoming waves of applause could be heard
the sound of the violin starting a new melody. The Count's feet took
him in the direction of the sound for two or three short blocks; he
walked along the wall of a large house located a little before the
approach to Hitotsubashi Bridge, then turned left and came to the
end of a small lane. There, in the midst of many closed and abandoned shops, was a three-story wooden house in Western style, its
lights shining brightly. Clearly, the violin and people clapping were
on the third floor of this house; in the room beyond the balcony,
with its tightly shut glass doors, a crowd must be gathered around

a table in the very midst of a banquet.

Count G. had no knowledge of or interest in music, particularly Chinese music, but as he stood beneath the balcony listening to the sound of the violin, its eerie melody stimulated his appetite, just as if it had been the smell of food cooking. The colors and textures of all the Chinese foods he knew came into his mind one after the other in time to the music. When the music quickened, the strings emitting a harsh sound like a young girl singing at the top of her lungs, it made the Count think somehow of the bright red color and sharp, strong flavor of dragonfish guts. And when suddenly the melody became full, rounded, and plaintive like a voice that is thick with tears, he thought of a rich broth of braised sea cucumbers, so full-flavored that each mouthful keeps permeating one's taste buds to their very roots. And when the final hail of applause came, he saw at once in his mind's eye all the many marvelously flavored varieties of Chinese cuisine, until finally even the empty soup bowls, fish bones, china spoons and cups, and even the grease-stained tablecloth appeared clearly before him.

Count G. licked his lips several times and swallowed the saliva that had accumulated in his mouth, but the need to eat that surged up from the pit of his stomach became quite unbearable. He thought he knew every single Chinese restaurant in Tokyo, and yet here was this one—how long had it been here? At any rate, it must have been some karma that had allowed him, drawn by the sounds of the Chinese violin, to discover it tonight. And if so, the food *had* to be worth trying at least once. Besides, he had a strong hunch that he would find in there some treat he'd never had before. . . . As he thought of this, his belly, which had felt quite replete until a few minutes before, suddenly drew itself in and gave him such a pang of hunger that the skin over the stomach was stretched tight. To his surprise, the Count's whole body now began to tremble, like a warrior of old standing at the head of his army before leading a charge.

The Count tried to open the door and go in, but was disappointed to find that it was shut tight, seemingly locked from inside. Moreover, having put his hand on the doorknob of what he'd assumed to be a restaurant, he noticed only now that there was a sign hung by the door with the words "Chechiang Hall" on it. The sign was made of plain, weather-worn wood, and the black writing looked as if it had been exposed to a lot of rain. The name of the hall was inscribed in these rather faded but large, bold characters, in a typically Chinese hand. Since the Count was thinking of nothing but food, it was no wonder he hadn't noticed the signboard; yet had he paid some heed to the outward appearance of the building, he should have known in advance that it was not a restaurant. If it had been a Chinese restaurant like those in Kanda or Yokohama's Chinatown, he would have seen hunks of pork, whole roast chickens, jellyfish, and smoked meats hanging in front of the place; and the door of course would have been wide open. But as just mentioned, the ground-floor door facing the street was closed, as were the windows. And since in addition the door was not of glass but a painted louver shutter, it was impossible to see anything inside. Only the third floor was lively with sounds; the windows of the second floor were completely dark. There was only one dim light at the edge of the eaves just above the entrance, shedding its uncertain light on the signboard and its inscription. There was also a bell on the side of the door opposite the signboard, with the words "Night Bell" written in English and "Those on business should ring here" in Japanese on a white piece of paper about the size of a calling card. However, no matter how much the Count might long for the food to be obtained inside, he hadn't the courage to go ahead and ring the bell. This Chechiang Hall must be a club for Chinese residents of Japan originally from that province. He couldn't just burst in and ask to be made a party to their feast. Such were his thoughts as he stood there, his face pressed tenaciously against the metal door.

The kitchen, it seemed, was near the entrance, and from the cracks around the metal door a warm fragrance escaped, like steam rising from those wooden steamers used in making *dim-sum* snacks. It occurred to the Count that his face probably resembled that of a cat crouching on the kitchen floor, intent on snatching the fish being prepared by the sink. If he could, he would gladly have turned into a cat and crept into the house and licked the used plates and bowls one after the other. But there was no point now in lamenting the fact that he had not been born a cat. "Tsk," he said regretfully, then wetly licked his lips and moved away from the door with obvious reluctance.

Isn't there some *way I can manage to try the food here?* Standing there with the sounds of the violin and applause raining down on him from the upper floor, he found it hard to give up, and began walking back and forth along the lane. The truth was, from the moment he realized it was *not* a restaurant, his desire to sample the food here had burned all the more fiercely. This wasn't only out of eagerness to impress the other club members by discovering an unexpectedly interesting place in such an unlikely part of town. It was knowing that this was a club for Chinese from Chechiang Province, that there they were, enjoying real Chinese food as they listened to that intoxicating music, exactly following the customs of their native land—it was this that piqued his interest. As he would have been the first to admit, he'd never tasted real Chinese cooking yet. He had often experienced the dubious Chinese fare to be found in restaurants all over Tokyo and Yokohama; but that was usually based on poor ingredients cooked in a semi-Japanese style. According to people who had traveled there, the food one was served in China was of a different order altogether, and he'd long suspected that such authentic Chinese food was precisely the ideal cuisine the members of the Gourmet Club were dreaming of. So if this Chechiang Hall was, as he supposed, a place where a purely Chinese style of life prevailed, it might be the grail he'd been seeking. On top of the tables there on the upper floor he imagined rows of the sort of masterworks he'd been struggling to create for years—a dazzling artistry of tastes, shedding its brilliance on the scene. To the accompaniment of the Chinese violin, a full orchestra of flavors, resonant with luxury and pleasure, would be sounding forth, swaying the very souls of the guests who filled the room. The Count knew that in all China the Chechiang area was the richest in ingredients for a fine cuisine. Whenever he heard the word Chechiang, he recalled it as a mystic realm of scenic beauty on the banks of the Western Lake, famed in the poetry of Po Lo-t'ien and Su Tung-p'o. And also as the best place for Sungari sea bass and for pork belly cooked in soy à la Tung-p'o.

He had been standing under the eaves for around thirty minutes, allowing his taste buds to come to full bloom there, when he sensed someone heavily descending the stairway from the second floor. Soon a Chinese fellow emerged unsteadily from the doorway. He must have been very drunk, for as he came out he staggered and bumped against the Count's shoulder. "Aah!" he cried, which was followed by what must have been a few words of apology in Chinese. Then, apparently realizing the other person was Japanese, he shifted languages, saying very distinctly "Excuse me." He was a stout man of close to thirty, wearing the cap of a Tokyo Imperial University student; though he had duly apologized, he stared at the stranger for some moments with an air of intense suspicion at finding him in such a place.

"No, no, it's I who should apologize. You see, I'm very fond of Chinese food; and the smells coming from inside were so good that I forgot myself and have just been standing here enjoying them!" This naively candid statement that came so readily to the Count's lips made a great hit with his hearer. Ordinarily, he would never have been up to doing this, but no doubt his sincerity—his profound seriousness when it came to gastronomical matters—had moved Heaven itself. His way of saying it must have been rather amusing, for the student's plump belly began to shake with approving laughter.

"No, really, eating good food is my greatest pleasure in life, and everyone knows Chinese food is the best in the world!"

"Ha-ha-ha," the Chinese continued good-naturedly.

"And you know, I've been to every single Chinese restaurant in Tokyo; but what I've actually been wanting to try is some *genuine* Chinese food, not restaurant food but the sort served in a place like this, for Chinese people only. So, what about it? I know it seems awfully forward of me, but I wonder if you couldn't let me join your party tonight and try some of the food here. Let me introduce myself. . . ," he said, producing a calling card from a small case.

This dialogue seemed to have drawn the attention of the guests on the upper floor. Five or six men came down one after another and surrounded the Count. Others just opened the door halfway and stuck their heads out to have a look. In the dark lane, the area under the eaves was suddenly flooded with light from inside the building, and the impressive figure of the Count, in his heavy overcoat, with his plump red cheeks, stood out clearly. Amusingly, the numerous Chinese who surrounded him all displayed the same sort of bulging cheeks, which glistened in the light as they grinned at him.

"Fine, fine! Please come in. We'll give you a proper Chinese dinner!" someone called out shrilly, sticking his head out of one of the third-floor windows. A burst of laughter and applause rose from among his companions both above and below.

"The food here is extremely good—very different from what you get at an ordinary restaurant. You'll be delighted!" said another man from among those surrounding the Count in a tempting voice.

"Come on, then, don't hang back! Go up and eat your fill!" Everyone in the group spoke drunkenly and half in fun, their breath carrying the strong smell of rice wine. The Count, feeling somewhat dazed, as if all this might be a dream, trooped in along with the rest. In the room just inside the metal door, which had looked pitch-dark from outside, a light whose shade had glass bead tassels hanging from it shone brightly. A shelf to the right held green plums, jujubes, longans, and mandarin oranges, as well as various canned goods. Beside the shelf hung chunks of pork loin and pigs' legs with the skin still on. The bristles had been carefully shaved off, and the skin was as soft, white, and luscious as any woman's. On the facing wall beyond the shelf was a lithograph of a beautiful Chinese woman. Nearby, a small window had been set into the wall, and through it great gusts of smoke and cooking smells came flooding into the small room, making the air thick. No doubt the kitchen was just beyond, as the Count had imagined. But he had time for only a glance at all this as he was guided to the steep staircase near the front door and immediately led up to the second floor. This floor was very oddly arranged. Having climbed the staircase, one came to a narrow corridor with a white wall along one side and a partition of blue-painted wood along the other. The partition was less than six feet in height, some two to three feet lower than the ceiling, and must have been about seventeen or eighteen feet long. Every six feet or so there was a small, low door. Just inside each of the three doors hung a drab, dirty-looking curtain of white cotton, as if one were backstage in a cheap theater. When the Count reached this floor, the curtain of the middle door moved and parted as a young woman stuck her head out. With her round, chubby face (almost uncannily white), her large eyes and snub nose, she resembled a little Pekinese. Frowning, she stared at the Count suspiciously; then, showing a flash of gold tooth, she screwed her lips up, spat a watermelon seed onto the floor, and drew her head back inside the curtain.

Why would they divide up such a small space into rooms like this? And what is that woman behind the curtain up to? The Count had barely time to frame such questions to himself before he was led further up the staircase, to the third floor.

Meanwhile the smoke from the downstairs kitchen climbed up the staircase, narrow as a chimney, just behind the Count. It rose to the very ceiling of the third-floor room to which he was now guided. He had been so thoroughly "smoked" as he ascended the stairs that he felt as if his body had been roasted *à la Chinoise*. But the room he entered was filled not only with the fumes from the kitchen but also with tobacco smoke, perfume, steam, carbon dioxide, and various other smells all jumbled together. The atmosphere was so heavy, with a sort of gray haze to it, that one couldn't clearly distinguish people's faces. The first things that the Count noticed, after being brought in so suddenly from the dark, quiet lane outside, were this hazy atmosphere and the strangely humid closeness of the place.

A man who had come forward from among the group that had

guided him there shouted, purposely using Japanese: "Gentlemen, I wish to introduce to you all Count G!"

The Count came to himself and removed his hat and coat, which were immediately snatched from him by five or six hands on either side and carried off somewhere. Then one of the men took him by the hand and led him in front of one of the tables. By now he could see that he was in one very large room which had not been divided into cubicles like the second floor. Two big round tables stood in the center, with perhaps fifteen or more diners seated at each, all making an assault on a great big beauty of a bowl placed in the middle, all plying their spoons, thrusting with their chopsticks, vying with one another to gorge themselves on the food inside it. The Count was only able to steal a glance or two, but it seemed that one of the bowls contained a soup so thick and heavy that it looked like melted clay, in which rested (and there could be no doubt of it) an unborn piglet, boiled whole. It preserved the original form of the animal, but what emerged from beneath the skin was something soft and spongy, rather like boiled fishcake and quite unlike cooked pork. Moreover, both the skin and its contents had apparently been boiled so long they were as soft as jelly, so that merely by inserting a spoon one came away with a mouthful, just as if one had used a sharp carving knife. As the Count watched, spoons were thrust in from every side, and the original form of the piglet disappeared chunk by chunk, from the outside inward, as if by magic.

The bowl on the other table clearly contained swallow's nest soup. People kept reaching their chopsticks in and scooping up pieces of bird's nest as slippery as jelly-noodles. What was unusual was the pure white soup in which the swallow's nest was steeping. The Count had never seen any liquid so white as this in all his experience of Chinese food, apart from the medicinal "apricot water" concoction; but he'd heard that if one went to China one might be served a kind of "milk soup," and he wondered if this wasn't it.

It was not, however, to one of these two tables that the Count was being directed. For along both facing walls there were raised platforms, like those to be found in the meditation hall at a Zen temple. Here too a number of people were sitting around small sandalwood tables placed here and there. Some were sitting directly on the floor, others on damask mats; some were smoking brass water pipes, others sipping tea from cups made in Ching-te-chen. All were sunk in an impassive silence, gazing absently at the busy goings-on at the central tables with weary eyes in slack, sleepy faces. And yet not one of them looked ill, or seedy, or shabby. All were fine-looking men, well-built, with healthy faces; only, they seemed abstracted, as if some inner focus had been lost.

Aha, this bunch have just finished stuffing themselves, and they're taking a break. Judging by their sleepy look, they must have overeaten quite a bit.

Actually, that "sleepy look" filled the Count with envy. Those swollen stomachs must be crammed with delicious things, bones and guts all turned to mush, just like the whole boiled piglet's fetus in the soup. Yes, if one broke the skin of their bellies, what would flow out would not be blood or intestines but Chinese foods all stewed together, as in those bowls set upon the tables. To judge from the sated, listless expressions on their faces, they might go on sitting there, calmly at their ease, even if their bellies *were* burst open.

The Count and the other Gourmet Club members had also eaten their way to a point beyond satiation any number of times; but he felt that he had never yet known the grand satisfaction that was evident on the faces of these assembled men.

He passed along in front of them, but they merely glanced at him:

no one showed either a trace of suspicion or a sign of welcome at the intrusion of this unfamiliar guest. No doubt it would have seemed just too bothersome to them even to wonder what this Japanese was doing here.

Eventually, the person leading him stopped in front of a gentleman who sat leaning against the wall in a corner to the left. This fellow too had, of course, eaten his fill and more, and sat smoking, his eyes wide open in a vacant, invalid's stare. Being fat, he looked younger than his years, but he must have been close to forty and was apparently the most senior member of the dining club. While the others were mostly in Western dress, he alone was wearing a black satin Chinese robe with a squirrel-fur lining.

What drew the Count's attention, however, was not so much the appearance of the man as the presence to his left and right of two beautiful women. One was wearing an overrobe with broad, deep green vertical stripes against a celadon-colored background, with short trousers to match. Over silk stockings of pale pink she wore on her dainty feet purple sateen slippers exquisitely embroidered in silver thread. She sat in a chair with her right foot crossed over her left knee, and the foot was so small and charming it looked like one of those little accessory cases that girls often carry in the breast of their kimono. Her lustrous black hair, parted in the middle at the front, fell like a reed blind to her eyebrows. From her earlobes, which could be glimpsed like little acorns behind her tresses, hung earrings of jade, swaying and shining with a soft green light. It must have been she who was playing the music that the Count had heard a while ago. With the Chinese violin on her lap, held by her braceleted left hand, she looked like an image of the goddess Benzaiten. The woman's face was as smooth and pale as jade, and her large, dark, slightly protuberant eyes and full red upper lip, turned slightly upward toward her nose, had a certain enigmatic fascination about them. But most appealing of all were her teeth. Occasionally she would take a toothpick to the space on one side of her upper right canine, revealing her gums and clicking her upper and lower teeth together a bit as she did so—it *must* have been in order to display this dazzling set of teeth.

The other woman had a slightly long face, but she too was very beautiful. Perhaps because she was wearing a dark brown dress with an embroidered peony design, and a pearl brooch at the collar, the whiteness of her skin stood out all the more. She too was showing off her teeth, holding a toothpick and vigorously employing it with the fingers of her right hand, on one of which was a golden ring with five or six tiny bells dangling from it.

When the Count was brought before them, the two women turned aside, pretending not to notice him, and seemed to exchange meaningful glances with the gentleman who sat between them.

"This is Mr. Chen, our president," said the man who had led the Count by the hand, by way of introduction. He then proceeded to say something in very fast Chinese accompanied by a variety of gestures. The president made no reply either positive or negative, but sat silently listening, just blinking his eyes and looking as if he were about to yawn.

At last, though, he smiled briefly and spoke: "So you are Count G? I see. Everyone here is drunk, you know, which explains their bad manners. If you like Chinese food, we'll be glad to offer you some. But the food here now isn't very good. And besides, the kitchen has closed for the night. I'm very sorry, but I suggest you come again, to our next party." His response was quite clearly reluctant.

"No, no, you needn't prepare anything special for me! I know I shouldn't ask, but I'd be most grateful if you'd just let me try some of tonight's leftovers. Do you think that might be possible?"

If the man had shown a slightly more amiable, accommodating attitude, the Count would gladly have been more insistent still, adopting the wheedling tones of a beggar if necessary. Having caught sight of what was on those tables, he could hardly leave the place without at least a spoonful or two for himself.

"Ah, but you see what gluttons they all are—I'm afraid there'll *be* no leftovers. Anyway, it would be too rude to offer you our leavings. As president, I could never allow such a thing."

As he spoke, a frown of displeasure began to deepen on his brow, and he said several sharp words to the person standing alongside the Count. He emphasized this with a mocking glance and a thrust of his chin in the Count's direction, which seemed to mean "Get this Japanese out of here, now!" The other man looked crestfallen and apparently tried to say something in extenuation, but the president just sat there haughtily, blowing bursts of air through his nostrils, and showed no signs of giving in.

The Count ventured a brief glance over his shoulder and saw two waiters in the process of bringing two new bowls to the center tables, holding them high in the air. In the round, shallow china bowls, which were as big as basins, was an amber-colored soup that gave off puffs of steam as it sloshed about, almost overflowing the edge. One of the bowls contained a large piece of something that had been boiled to a dark, liverish color and appeared to be slimy, like a slug. It was still boiling away, there in its shallow "bath." When it was at last placed in the middle of the table, one of the diners stood up and raised a cup of *shao-hsing* wine, whereupon those sitting with him also rose and, all together, drained their cups. The minute they'd finished drinking, they then grasped their spoons, took up their chopsticks, and fell upon the bowls of broth. The Count, watching breathlessly, felt as if he were about to choke from frustration.

"I don't know what to say. I'm awfully sorry. The president just won't permit it. . . ." Scratching his head, the Chinese who had received the scolding reluctantly guided the Count toward the exit. "It was all our fault—we were drunk and dragged you up here. The president isn't a bad man, but he can be difficult at times."

"Oh no, I'm the one who's causing all the trouble. But I wonder *why* he won't give permission. Having actually seen this splendid dinner with my own eyes, I really do regret not being able to take part. . . . Is it absolutely necessary to have his permission?"

"Yes, since he's in charge of everything to do with this hall. . . ." As he said this, the man looked around to see if anyone was listening, but the two of them were already in the corridor, near the head of the stairs. "I think it's because he's suspicious of you. It isn't true that the kitchen's closed. Look—they're still at it down there, as you can see." And indeed the same puffs of fragrant smoke were rising from below. The sound of something being fried in a pan mingled with the sound of oil spattering—it was as lively as firecrackers going off. Along both sides of the corridor, the walls were still covered with a mass of dark coats, the guests showing no signs of leaving anytime soon.

"So the president thinks I'm a dubious character, eh? Well, it's only natural. Here I come wandering into this back lane without any particular business, and lurk about in front of the hall. No wonder he finds me suspicious. Why, I find it odd myself! However, I do have my reasons, which are hard to understand without some explanation. You see, we've formed this Gourmet Club. . . ."

"What? What kind of club is it?" He bent his head to one side, looking puzzled.

"Gourmet, a Gourmet Club—a 'Gastronomers' Club' they would call it in English."

"Oh really? I see, I see," said the other, nodding with a friendly smile.

"In other words, it's a club devoted to eating fine foods. All the members are people who can't live a day without eating something really good. But lately we've run out of things to try, and we don't know what to do. We split up every day and hunt through Tokyo for something a bit special, but there's nothing new or unusual to be had anywhere. Today too I was out on the prowl when I happened to find this place—I thought it was an ordinary Chinese restaurant when I came down the lane. So you see, I'm really not a suspicious character at all. The person on the card I gave you is indeed me. It's just that when it comes to food, I lose control of myself, forget all commonsense!"

The Chinese looked hard at the Count's face for a while as the latter went on making earnest excuses. "Is he mad?" perhaps he was thinking to himself. Tall and good-looking, with shiny pink cheeks probably due to drink, he was an honest-looking fellow of around thirty.

"I personally am not the least suspicious of you, sir," he said. "We—by which I mean all of us gathered here upstairs tonight—can understand your feelings perfectly. We don't call ourselves a 'Gourmet Club,' but in fact we get together here for exactly the same purpose: to eat delicious food. Like you, we're all keen 'gastronomers.'" At this point, he suddenly gave the Count's hand a good hard squeeze; then, with a significant look playing in his eyes, he went on: "I've spent two or three years in both America and Europe, and I learned that, no matter where you go in the world, you'll find nothing to match our Chinese cooking. I can't praise it too highly. And it's not because I'm Chinese. As a true 'gastronomer,' I believe you'll agree with me on this point—in fact, I'm sure of it. You told me about your club; and so, as proof that I really do trust you, I'll tell you about *our* club—about this hall. They serve some highly original things here. What you saw there on the tables, that was just the beginning, the prologue to our dinner. The real feast is still to come."

He gazed quizzically at the Count's face, as if to see what reaction his words had produced, though he must have known they were bound to tantalize him.

"Is that true? Or are you having a little joke at my expense?" By now there was a wild look in the Count's eyes, like a hound on the scent of its prey. "If it is true, then I want to ask you one more favor. It's just too cruel to let me hear that much and then send me away like this! Please explain to your president once again that I am *not* a suspicious character. And if that doesn't clear up his doubts, then test me to see if I'm a gourmet or not, right in front of him. Chinese food or whatever, I will identify the flavor of each and every dish to be found up to now in Japan. Then he'll realize what a fanatic I am about food. Incidentally, I find it rather odd that he should dislike us Japanese so much. You said it was a dining club, but I wonder if it might not be a political meeting of some kind!"

"A political meeting? Not at all." The Chinese laughed, flatly dismissing the suggestion. "But as a club" (and here he suddenly became serious, speaking slowly and spacing his words)—"I can say this because I have the utmost confidence in you, and in your title—as a club we are far more particular about who may join than any political group would be. The special dishes that are served in this hall are completely different from ordinary cooking. The ways of preparing them are kept an absolute secret from all non-members. . . . The group here tonight are mostly Chechiang people, but coming from Chechiang doesn't guarantee admission, by any means. It all depends on the president: the menu, the arrangements for the meeting place, the day set for the banquet, the expenses—everything is subject to his decision. This club is, in fact, *his* club, you might say...."

"Then, just what kind of person is this president of yours? Why does he have so much power?"

"He's a very strange man. He's admirable in many ways, but a bit stupid in others." The Chinese seemed to hesitate for a moment, mumbling to himself. Since the dining room was very noisy, their little chat, fortunately, would pass unnoticed.

"What do you mean by 'a bit stupid'?" When the Count urged him on like this, it was apparent from the look on the man's face that he regretted having gone so far. Then, clearly wondering whether he should speak further or not, he continued with some reluctance.

"Well, you see, he loves good food, to the point where it makes him act like a fool or a madman at times. And it's not just eating that he likes: he's also very good at preparing food. Now Chinese cooking involves a great variety of ingredients, but when he has a hand in it, there's nothing that can't be used. All kinds of vegetables, fruits, meat, fish, and birds, of course—everything, in fact, from the human down to the insect world can serve as an ingredient. As you know, from ancient times we Chinese have eaten swallow's nests. We've eaten shark's fins, bear's paws, deer's hoof sinews. But our president was the first to show us how to eat tree bark, and bird droppings, and human saliva. And various ways of boiling and roasting were discovered by him. As a result, where we might have had a little over ten types of soup before, now we have sixty or seventy. Another amazing innovation was in the things used to hold the food. Plates and bowls and jars and spoons made of china, porcelain, and metal —the president made it clear to us that these weren't the only possible kinds of tableware. And the food needn't always be placed inside a dish; it can also be smeared all over the outside. Or it can be spewed out over the dish, like a fountain. And there could even be times when you might not be able to tell which was the food and which the container! Without going that far, you can't really claim to know what the finest cuisine is—that's our president's opinion."

". . . Having told you this much, I'm sure you can form a general idea of the kind of things he devises for us. And you should be able to understand why we're so selective about who can join our group and attend our dinners. Because if this sort of cooking ever became at all popular, it would lead to worse things than if smoking opium became the rage, you see?"

"Well, let me ask again then: is the menu that's about to be served tonight typical of its kind?"

"Yes, you might say so." The Chinese, coughing as if choking on his cigar smoke, gave a slight nod.

"I understand. I can imagine what's involved from your description. With a dining club like yours, it's only natural that you should be more strictly selective even than a secret political society. To tell the truth, my own epicurean ideal has always been similar to your president's, the big difference being that he—to his great credit— seems to know how to attain it. But, even given the strict selection criteria, I wonder why, if he's so intent on maintaining secrecy, he doesn't limit the number of members more. If it's just a matter of eating, why shouldn't he limit it to one person—himself?"

"No, he has his reasons there too. He believes that you can't bring out the best in an elaborate meal without having a really large number of people present—it has to be done that way. So, while he's very particular in choosing the participants, he also insists on assembling plenty of them, as you can see tonight. . . ."

"I agree with him on that as well. My own club has only five members, and when I compare that with tonight's gathering, I can see on how much greater a scale your president does things. I suppose it's because I'm so keen on good cooking, but I'm forever dreaming about it; and coming here tonight is just like a waking dream to me. Day and night I've been longing to encounter a man like that—the ultimate connoisseur. You said a few moments ago that you trusted me completely, and I'm sure you've spoken so freely because you *do* trust me. Certainly you know by now how serious I am. So, couldn't you go just one step further and try recommending me to your president one more time? If he still absolutely refuses, then, even if I can't sit at the table and eat, mightn't it be possible for me to hide in the shadows somewhere and at least *see* what the meal's like?"

Count G. spoke so passionately that it was hard to believe it was a discussion of something as commonplace as food.

"What can we do?. . ." The Chinese seemed to have sobered up completely. He stood there perplexed, lost in thought, with his arms folded across his chest. Then, tossing on the floor the cigar he'd been smoking, he raised his head, apparently having come to some decision. "I've already done my best to be helpful . . . but you seem to have set your heart on it, so I don't want to disappoint you. But there's no hope of getting the president's permission, however good the recommendation. For all I know, he may think you're from the police. It would be better to say nothing to him and just have a quiet look for yourself."

He looked down the corridor to make sure there was no one watching, then suddenly extended a hand and gave a strong push to the wooden door against which he'd been leaning as he spoke. A section of the door, which was covered with overcoats, easily and soundlessly opened inward, and the two of them were drawn into the shadowy interior. The room they found themselves in was tightly sealed on all four sides by plain, rough wood paneling. There were two tired-looking couches, one on each side, with tea tables on which were placed ashtrays and matches at the head of each couch. Apart from that there was nothing, no decorations or other furnishings. A strange odor filled the room.

"What is this room used for? It has a very odd smell."

"Don't you recognize it? It's opium," said the Chinese calmly, with an unpleasant little laugh. His appearance had changed, as if he were another person, perhaps due to the shadow across half his face, cast by the dim light of a lamp with a green shade set in one corner of the room. Even his eyes, which up to now had seemed friendly and sincere, had a languid, dissolute look to them—the look of a ruined race.

"I see. It's a place for smoking opium in, is it?"

"Yes. You're probably the first Japanese who's ever been in here. Even the Japanese employees don't know it exists." He seemed completely relaxed, entirely trusting. He sat down on one of the couches and then, as if it were his custom, sprawled out there, his voice taking on the low, lifeless tone of someone in an opium haze. "Ahh, the smell's quite strong! Somebody must have been smoking here a little while ago. Look—there's a little hole in the paneling. If you peek through, you can see everything that's going on in the dining room. People come in here to look at the scene next door and then slowly float off into dreamland."

The author owes it to the reader to describe all that went on at the banquet in the next room, as viewed by Count G. through the hole in the wall of the opium den. Yet, just as the organizer of that event felt it necessary to make a strict selection of the participants, so too I would need to be strict in my choice of reader. And since that is impossible to do, I regret to say that I cannot record the naked facts of what went on that night. So let me just report the extent to which the Count's long-cherished dreams were satisfied, and afterward how much progress he was able to make in the talent and creativity he brought to culinary events—and all because of what he saw that night. In fact, shortly after that episode, he won the highest praise and loudest applause ever given by the members of his club, who acknowledged him as a great epicurean, indeed a genius of fine cuisine. Not knowing the facts of the case, they all without exception wondered from whom the Count had inherited the gift of this type of cooking, or how he had managed to discover it overnight. The astute nobleman, however, mindful of the promise he'd made to the Chinese, not only kept the existence of the Chechiang Hall a complete secret but stoutly asserted that the new cuisine was the result of his own creative impulses.

"I haven't learned it from anyone, it's all due to inspiration!" he insisted with an air of innocence.

Every night in the upper-floor dining room of the Gourmet Club a truly amazing banquet was held under the auspices of the Count. The dishes that appeared on the table for the most part resembled Chinese food, yet in some respects they were unprecedented. And as the first banquet was followed by the second, and that by the third, the types of food and methods of preparation grew richer and richer, more and more complex. Let me list here the menu for the first night, in the order in which the dishes appeared: Swallow's Nest Soup; Chicken Gruel with Shark's Fins; Hoof Sinews with Sea Cucumbers; Whole Roast Duck; Assorted Fried Meats; "Dragon Playing with Spheres" (steamed snake with quail eggs); Ham with Chinese Cabbage; Sliced Yams in Hot Sugared Syrup; "Petals of Jade Orchids" (dried bamboo shoots); "Paired Winter Bamboo Shoots."

Seeing a list like this, there will be those who come to the hasty conclusion that this is fairly standard Chinese food. And to be sure, these names for dishes are commonplace in that cuisine. The club members too, when they first read the menu, all thought to themselves: "What? More Chinese stuff?" But their discontent lasted only till the moment when the dishes were brought forward. For what was at last set before them was for the most part utterly different from what they'd imagined from the menu, not only in taste but even in outward form.

For example, the Chicken Gruel with Shark's Fins was neither a gruel made from any ordinary chicken nor one that contained the fins of sharks. A huge silver bowl was filled to the brim with a wonderfully hot broth—thick, opaque as *yōkan* sweet-bean jelly, and heavy as melted lead. Stimulated by the heady aroma emanating from the bowl, the guests plunged their spoons greedily into the broth. But when they put it into their mouths, to their surprise only a sweet winelike flavor diffused itself; no taste of shark's fins or chicken gruel was apparent.

"What's this supposed to be? And what's so damn good about it? It's just sickeningly sweet, that's all!" one of the more quick-tempered members said. But no sooner were the words spoken than the look on his face began gradually to change, as if he'd just thought of something very strange indeed, or even actually discovered it; and his eyes suddenly opened wide in a shocked stare. For he found that the sweetness of which he'd just been complaining was now giving way to hints of chicken gruel and shark's fins, gently permeating his tongue.

The sweet broth had certainly been swallowed, but its effects had by no means ended with that. The winelike sweetness that had spread throughout his mouth had indeed grown gradually fainter but still lingered at the base of the tongue. Then all at once the broth that had just been swallowed came surging back into the oral cavity in the form of a belch. And, wondrously, the taste of chicken gruel and fish fins accompanied the belch. No sooner had they combined with the sweetness that still remained on the tongue than an indescribably fine flavor emerged. Wine and chicken and shark's fins met together in the mouth and fermented, the effect now being something close to *shiokara* salted fish guts. As the number of belches increased from one to two to three, the flavors grew richer and more pungent.

"Well, how about it? It's not just sickeningly sweet now, is it?" The Count surveyed the faces of the men around him and allowed himself a satisfied smirk. "You mustn't think you're meant to enjoy the sweet taste of the broth. What I want you to taste is the belch that comes afterward. You eat the sweet soup so as to enjoy the belch. The first thing to do for people like us who are always overeating is to eliminate the unpleasantness of belching. Food that leaves you with an unpleasant sensation after eating can't be called true *haute cuisine*, no matter how good the initial flavor may be. No—a dish where, the more you eat of it, the more delectable the belches that follow become—that's the sort of food we can fill our stomachs with and never get tired of! What you've just been eating isn't all that unusual, but I think I can recommend it to you with confidence on that point."

"Well, I *am* impressed. After a triumph like this, you certainly are entitled to the prize money." The man who'd just been attacking the Count was now the first to compliment him, and the rest of the group were even more effusive in their praise.

"Couldn't we perhaps get you to tell us all just how you managed to create such a marvelous dish? We'll always be wondering how on earth a belch like that could result from that too-sweet broth of yours."

"No, that's one thing I'm afraid I can't do. If my discovery were a simple matter of cooking, I might well feel obliged to pass it on, as one member of the Gourmet Club to another. But it's not so much cookery as magic. Gastronomical magic! And accordingly I prefer to keep the method of preparation secret, as is my right. So I leave it to your imaginations, gentlemen." The Count smiled at them pityingly.

However, the "gastronomical magic" was not limited only to what I have just described. Each of the various dishes on the menu assaulted the club members' taste buds from an unexpected direction, and all were the products of utterly different tastes and conceptions. "Taste buds," did I say? That may not do justice to the case. Actually, the members were able truly to savor the various dishes only after having employed every one of the senses they were endowed with. They did not merely taste the cuisine with their tongues: they had to taste it with their eyes, their noses, their ears, and at times with their skin. At the risk of exaggerating, every part of them had to become a tongue.

The Ham with Chinese Cabbage in particular might be said to be the best example of this. Chinese cabbage is a vegetable similar to ordinary cabbage, with a thick white stem. But at first taste this dish too, like the others, did not have the flavors of ham or a vegetable, and it was the last to appear, after all the other main dishes on the menu had been served. Before it was brought out, the members were required first to move five or six feet away from the table and then to stand scattered apart around the room. With the windows and doors carefully sealed so that not even a particle of light could seep in from any aperture, however small, all the lights were suddenly turned off. The interior of the room was made so pitch-dark that one couldn't see even an inch ahead. In that soundless, dead-quiet darkness the members were made to stand in absolute silence for some thirty minutes.

The reader must try to imagine their feelings then. They had eaten too much. Even if they weren't afflicted with any nasty burping, their stomachs were swollen with food. Their limbs were weighed down with the heavy lethargy that comes from overfullness. Their nervous systems were numbed, and they felt drowsy, almost on the verge of sleep. Now, suddenly plunged into darkness and made to stand for so long, their nerves, which had begun to go dull, became acute again. The thought "What will come next? What will we be fed in the dark like this?" rose strongly within them, bringing a good deal of tension with it. The stove had of course been turned off to exclude all light, and the place was getting colder; all sleepiness had vanished without a trace. Their eyes, in the darkness in which nothing could be seen, strained to open wider. In short, they were in a state of heightened awareness before they could even taste the next dish.

Just when such feelings had reached their highest pitch, they heard the sound of someone's footsteps stealthily approaching from one corner of the room. It was clear from the sensuous swish of silk that it was not one of the people who'd been in the room before. Judging by the light, graceful sound of slippers, it must have been a woman. They couldn't tell how she had entered the room, or from where; but this person silently paced from one end of the room to the other, like a wild animal in a cage, passing just in front of the club members as she did so, five or six times. This went on for perhaps two or three minutes. Soon the footsteps, which had moved to the right side of the room, came to a stop in front of one of the members who had been made to stand there. . . . I shall call this man "A.," and try to explain what happened next from A.'s point of view. Until it was their turn, nothing happened for a while to anyone else.

A. felt sure that the person whose footsteps had just stopped in front of him was indeed, as he'd imagined, a woman. The reason was that the smells of hair oil and powder and perfume peculiar to women were now unmistakable. With her standing directly opposite him, her face all but rubbing against his own, A. found these smells almost suffocating as they enveloped him. The room's darkness was so thick that he couldn't see her, even so; he only knew of her presence by relying on the senses other than sight. Her soft hair brushed against his forehead. Her warm breath caressed his neck. Meanwhile, the woman's cool but soft palms stroked A.'s cheeks two or three times, up and down, up and down—the effect was uncanny.

Judging from the fleshiness of her palms and the suppleness of her fingers, A. was sure that it was a young woman. However it wasn't clear to him just why those hands were rubbing his face. First they pressed against his right and left temples and rubbed them, then both palms were placed over his eyelids and began to stroke softly downward, repeatedly, as if to wear his eyeballs away. Next, they moved gradually to his cheeks and began to rub either side of his nose. There seemed to be several rings on both right and left hands, for he could feel the coldness of things small, hard, and metallic. . . . As A. yielded to this facial massage, he felt a refreshing physiological pleasure, as after a full cosmetic treatment, seeping down into the very core of his brain.

That sense of pleasure was greatly heightened by the still more delicate operation that took place immediately afterward. Having given A.'s face a thorough rubbing, those hands at last grasped his lips, stretching and releasing them like a rubber band. For a time the hands would rest on his chin and firmly rub his cheeks just over where the back teeth were. Then the fingertips would softly tap along the rims of his upper and lower lips, tapping their way all around. The fingers would move to the edges of his mouth and little by little induce his saliva to emerge, spreading it all over, until at last his lips were drenched with his own spittle. Over and over the fingertips rubbed themselves wetly along the crease of his still-closed lips. Though he had as yet eaten nothing, his lips felt as if his cheeks were already bulging with some substance that made his saliva come dribbling out like this. Naturally his appetite was aroused. The greedy saliva that urged him to gormandize welled up endlessly from behind his back teeth, filling his entire mouth. . . .

A. was unable to help himself: the drool was about to flow without any aid from those fingers. Just then, the woman's fingertips, which had been toying with his lips, were suddenly inserted inside. After rummaging about in the space between the inside of his lips and his gums, they gradually moved in the direction of his tongue. His saliva stickily enveloped those five fingers, transforming them into viscous things—fingers, or something else, it was hard to tell. What A. noticed then for the first time was how very soft and slippery they were: so tender it hardly seemed possible that they were part of a human body, no matter how long they might have been immersed in saliva. It ought to have been quite distressing to have five fingers thrust into one's mouth, yet A. felt no such distress. Or, if perhaps he did feel a little, it was no more than if a large glutinous rice cake had been stuffed into his mouth. If by accident he had brought his teeth down on them, it seemed likely the fingers would have been cut into several pieces.

All at once A. felt that his saliva, which was sticking to that hand as well as to his tongue, had begun for some reason to have a peculiar taste. A sweetish flavor with an aromatic, salty undertaste was gradually emerging from within the spittle. How could saliva have a taste like this? Or, for that matter, how could a woman's hand? A. moved his tongue around and lapped up the flavor. The more he licked and tasted, the more flavor emerged from somewhere or other. Finally he swallowed all the saliva in his mouth, but still a strange liquid welled up on the surface of his tongue, as if being squeezed from something drop by drop. By now A. had to admit the fact that it must be coming from between the woman's fingers. Nothing apart from her hand had entered his mouth from outside. And that hand, with its five fingers, had been resting on his tongue, unmoving, for some time. The slick fluid that clung to those fingers had certainly seemed until now to be A.'s own saliva; yet from the fingers themselves as well, a sticky, saliva-like liquid was being slowly exuded, like an oily sweat.

But what could this slippery stuff be? It's something I've tasted before. I know I've had this kind of thing before, somewhere. A. thought the matter over even as he licked away at the fingers with the tip of his tongue. Then it came to him: it was somehow similar to the smell of the ham used in Chinese cooking. Actually, he may well have been aware of that for some time, but the conjunction was so unexpected that he hadn't been clearly conscious of it.

Yes, it definitely tastes like ham—and in particular, Chinese-style ham. To confirm this judgment, A. concentrated his sense of taste still more fully in the tip of his tongue and kept on licking and sucking persistently at those fingers. Strangely, the more pressure he applied with his tongue, the tenderer the fingers became, dissolving into shreds as leeks might, for example. Suddenly A. discovered that what had unmistakably been a human hand had somehow changed into the stem of a Chinese cabbage. No, perhaps "changed" isn't quite the word, for though it had the taste and feel of *bok choi*, it still perfectly preserved the shape of human fingers. In fact the second and middle fingers were still sporting rings, just as before. And the palm was still firmly connected to the flesh of the wrist. It was impossible to tell where the *bok choi* left off and the woman's hand began. It was, if you will, a kind of hybrid—"*Bok Choi* Fingers."

That was not the only mysterious thing. While A. was puzzling over all this, the *bok choi*—or human hand, whichever it was—started to move about inside his mouth as if it were a second tongue. Each of the five fingers began to move: one thrust itself into a cavity in one of his back teeth, another twined itself around his tongue, while yet another wedged itself between his upper and lower teeth, as if eager to be bitten. Insofar as it "moved," it was most certainly a human hand; but as it moved, it became increasingly clear that it was without question *bok choi*, composed of vegetable fiber. When A. gingerly bit into the tip of one, as if eating the head of an asparagus stem, it was immediately crushed, and the flesh of the crushed portion was transformed into real *bok choi*. Moreover, it was a tender sort of *bok choi*, like a well-boiled giant radish, sweeter and moister than anything he'd had before. Drawn on by the wondrous flavor, he bit down on each of the five fingertips, crushing them, and then swallowing. The fingers, however, not only lost nothing of their shape but continued to exude a liquid and to twine the *bok choi* fibers around his teeth and tongue. Bite down and chew as he might, from the tips of the fingers there sprouted endless replacements—just as a long string of little flags might emerge from within the hands of some stage magician.

Around the time A. felt that even one more of these delicious stems would be too much, the fingertips changed again from vegetable to authentic human flesh, then made a clean sweep of the leftover bits in his mouth, sprinkled among his teeth some tingling stimulant like peppermint, and smartly withdrew.

This was the final main dish at the first night's banquet. From the two examples given above, the reader should be able to imagine in a general way how very strange were the other things that appeared on the menu.

After the *bok choi*, the darkened hall was once again flooded with light; yet there was no trace or shadow of the woman to whom those mysterious hands must have belonged.

"With this, we bring tonight's meeting of the Gourmet Club to an end," said Count G. in a simple closing speech as he gazed at the amazed expressions on the faces of the assembled members. "I said earlier that tonight's menu would be no ordinary one, but a magical one. Yet I want to make it perfectly clear that I haven't resorted to magic merely out of eccentricity, or as a means of disguising the fact that I couldn't come up with a genuinely inventive meal. I honestly believe that there is no way to create a truly fine cuisine *without* using magic. The reason is that we already know the flavor of all those fine foods that can be tasted with the tongue alone. Within the limited range of what is called a 'cuisine,' there's nothing more to be found that can satisfy us. As a result, in order to provide ourselves with other satisfying tastes, we must both greatly expand the range of that 'cuisine' and also diversify as much as possible the senses we use in enjoying it. In order to fully develop our responses as gourmets, it is necessary for us first of all to focus our interest and curiosity fully on the thing to be eaten, and only afterward enjoy the flavors themselves. The more intense our curiosity, the more the value of the thing will increase. If I make use of magic in my cookery, it's because I want to excite such curiosity in all of you...."

The members looked dazed, and left the room without a word in reply, feeling as though they'd been bewitched by a fox.

The second banquet was held in the same meeting place on the following evening. I will spare the reader a full listing of the menu, only noting the name of the most unusual dish and explaining its contents, to wit:

Deep-fried Woman, Korean Style

On the first night's menu, the names of the dishes, if not their contents, were typical of purely Chinese cuisine, yet this was hardly the case here. One would of course have had no trouble recognizing "Fried Meat, Korean Style," as being Chinese, the words "Korean Style" in Chinese cooking referring to tempura: pork tempura, for example, is usually called "Korean Pork." But if one interpreted something called "Deep-fried Woman, Korean Style," in terms of Chinese food, it would have to mean literally the flesh of a woman, deep-fried as tempura. So it takes no great imagination to picture the excitement it aroused when the members of the club discovered this item on that evening's menu.

Now this dish was neither piled onto a plate nor poured into a bowl. It was wrapped in a single very large towel from which puffs of steam arose, and was borne reverently on the shoulders of three waiters, who placed it in the center of the table. Inside the towel was a beautiful girl dressed like a Chinese fairy, lying there smiling brightly. The angelic garment that covered her whole body seemed at first glance to be made of delicately patterned white damask. In actual fact, however, it was made entirely of deep-fried tempura batter; and so, in the case of this dish, the members tasted only the "robe" that clung to the girl's flesh.

～ ‖ ～

The above account offers no more than a peek at one small part of Count G.'s strange repertoire. His cuisine was too widely varied for us to be able to infer the whole from one part. Moreover, since his imagination was inexhaustible, no matter how detailed an account I might give of his many banquets, it would be impossible to know it in its entirety. I must, then, content myself with listing the names of the most exotic dishes from among the menus of the next four dinners, and then lay aside my pen. The list is as follows:

Pigeon-Egg Hot Springs
Fountain of Grapes
Phlegm-and-Spittle Liquid Jade
Snowy Pears, Petals and Peel
Braised Lips
Butterfly Broth
Velvet Carpet Soup
Crystal Tofu

I trust that among my wise readers there will be those who can infer what kind of content is implied by the names of these dishes. At any rate, the dinners of the Gourmet Club continue to be held every night at Count G.'s mansion. To all appearances, the members no longer merely "taste" or "eat" fine cuisine, but are "consumed" by it. And I for one believe that, in the not-too-distant future, this can only lead to two outcomes: either raving lunacy or death.

$\mathscr{M}$r. Bluemound

TRANSLATED BY
Paul McCarthy

Yurako had thought her husband, Nakada, had died of tuberculosis of the lungs. She still thought so, as did most people who knew him, but Nakada himself, it seemed, had thought differently. That much is clear from the will she found in the room where he breathed his last—the sickroom in the rented villa in Suma. But before I introduce the will itself in these pages, there is one thing I want the reader to know: namely, that Yurako's success as a rather well known film star was due not only to her undeniable physical charms but also in part to her dead husband. Nakada had picked her out right away from scores of fledgling starlets when she was just sixteen or seventeen and working as an extra with an appearance in one brief scene. He then used his position to do all he could to build her up. As so often happens in the movie business, there was a lot of jealous gossip about the love affair between the director and the actress, who began to live together openly when Yurako was eighteen. Probably at first, in addition to her real feelings for him, there was the ambition to make something of herself through him. Yet after the marriage she was never once unfaithful to him. They were to all appearances an enviably happy couple—so much so that it was even rumored that his gradual decline and death were due to an excess of loving attention from her.

She was a very healthy girl, and fond of exercise, and her lithe body burned with energy, so those rumors were perhaps not unreasonable. Even after her husband moved to Suma in the fall of last year, she would constantly visit him between shootings, and not necessarily just to nurse him through his illness, either. Her husband was physically weaker, but, as is often the case with patients of this sort, his sexual appetite was stronger than ever. It wasn't only that he eagerly awaited the supporting arms she willingly held out: imagine how grateful he must have been for that passion of hers which sucked love's pleasures to the last drop, without a trace of fear of infection from his disease.

It happened so often that Yurako herself must have thought she may have hastened her husband's death. But what of it, if he had welcomed that kind of death? And she herself had had little choice in the matter, since sexual desire smoldered in her body, too, just as it had in her husband's. One might have expected her to misbehave with someone else, but she hadn't done that: no, she had given him the sort of death he wished. She had joined the flame of her own spirit to his, which was about to vanish from this world, and fanned them to a blaze. Nakada must have left for the next world quite at peace, without regrets. Though he survived only four years after marrying this girl, he enjoyed those "springtime years"—from twenty-five to twenty-nine (while Yurako was eighteen to twenty-two)—without ever being betrayed by her, and without a single nasty spat between them.

Given her own temperament and plans for the future, however, Yurako can't have been unaware that his death was well timed, as a perfect ending to their affair. If he'd lived much longer, she couldn't have guaranteed her good behavior forever. She had by now built up quite a following among a certain set of fans, and was sure that she wouldn't be easily forgotten, even without the late director's patronage. After all, it was face and figure that were important in a film actress, not dramatic skill. No matter what the story or the script, it was enough if you remembered to show those beautiful teeth when you smiled, make your eyes glimmer through the tears when you cried, and give the audience a hint of flesh beneath the kimono during action scenes. They'd applaud all the more if you actually showed them some bare skin every now and then; for though they might say "She's no good—it's always the same old stuff," still, they loved to see it.

When Nakada made a movie with her, he always used the same technique. For a director to turn an actress (especially a woman he was in love with) into a star, it was less important to teach her acting skills than to dwell on each of her physical characteristics, of which he must acquire a firm knowledge, and to draw out the special qualities that would develop in the process. That was Nakada's theory. She had made all sorts of movies under his direction, but they were none of them "dramas" so much as simply a series of poses strung together, in which her young body was bathed in pools of light and streams of silk. All she had to do was impress the seal of that body on tens of thousands of feet of celluloid film, frame by frame. It was Nakada, in practice, who carved the markings on the seal, chose the vermilion ink with care, considered the proper placement, and pressed the seal firmly and clearly on the best quality paper.

Yurako would be grateful as long as she lived for the debt she owed her late husband. Still, once the seal-material had been certified as of good quality, the ink, the placement, and the paper could all take care of themselves; and there must be any number of good seal-carvers about. Besides, if the worst came to the worst, she knew her particular "seal-material" could be put to other uses. Thus her reaction to Nakada's death was not so much grief or dismay as a sense of having been able to work off her debt to some extent. In her sighs as she sat by his deathbed pillow, there was also a trace of something close to satisfaction, as of one who has successfully discharged a heavy responsibility. She had, if nothing else, safely seen her husband off to the next world. She didn't know what the future would hold for her, but she could gaze without any regrets at her husband's face, which, waxy white in death, looked noble and beautiful, and she could join her hands in prayer before him in the calm knowledge that her love for him had not yet begun to fade away.

Now, the will that I mentioned earlier emerged from a desk drawer when Yurako was moving out of the rented villa, taking her husband's ashes with her, but it was not till four or five days later that she read it. She hadn't realized at first that the octavo-sized volume wrapped in old newspaper was in fact a will; she hadn't in the least expected him to leave one. So it was really on a whim that she opened the heavily glued newspaper parcel. Under the first layer of paper there was yet another, on which was written in thick brushstrokes "For Yurako's Eyes Only." What emerged from the double wrappings of newsprint was a two-hundred-page volume that looked rather like an account book, with lines of gold scrollwork on its spine, and filled with spidery writing in pencil. The invalid must have kept it as a kind of journal of his illness whenever he had the time during the period of almost twelve months he spent, night and day, listening to the melancholy sound of the waves beating against the shore after his move to Suma. It was a very long account, and the pencil marks were sometimes very faint, having been rubbed away against the paper. Yurako had no idea what kind of confession her late husband might have made in this diary, and she approached it with some trepidation. But let the testament itself relate the strange matter that caused her, as she read, to shudder slightly; the facts that, as the dead man himself believed, had led directly to his death.

～ II ～

X Day, X Month, 19—

I want to set down here, beginning today, a record of something I intended never to divulge to you while I was alive. I do this because it's clear to me that I haven't much longer to live. When you left me last night, you did your best to encourage and comfort me; but afterward, alone, when I thought about my situation, there was no avoiding the fact that I was heading in a straight line to death. And that didn't make me frightened; on the contrary, I felt a kind of peace, a sense of resignation almost. Of course one regrets dying at the age of twenty-nine, but at least I had you in your young and beautiful prime. And when I think that I'm going to die while loved so deeply by you, my life doesn't seem such an unhappy one. You might answer that you're still only twenty-two, still in your best years; that you'll become even more beautiful, and love me even more. But it's time to tell you <u>what happened</u>, to tell you why I'm not really dying of tuberculosis but of something else. It was "what happened" that brought on this illness and robbed me of the will to live, and "what happened" will be the death of me. Reading about it won't be a pleasant experience for you, which is why I would still like to keep it from you. But I would feel too miserable dying without at least being honest with you. Some people might think it a peculiar reason for someone's death. Anyway, please take a look, since you're intimately involved in it all, as you will see when you read on.

It happened a long time ago, when I was still healthy, around the middle of May of the year before last, I think. It was a rainy evening, and I was having a Western dinner at the Green Café in Kyoto's Kyōgoku area, seated across from a man I'd never seen before. It was the day your *A Woman Who Loves Black Cats* first opened, and I was on my way home from seeing it at the Miyako Cinema together with Ikegami and Shiino. I was at the café by myself, though, since the other two had something to do elsewhere. The man was sitting there when I came in, and since the seat opposite happened to be empty, I sat down. For a while we just sat there in silence on either side of the table, but then I noticed he was looking at me with obvious interest, as if he wanted to speak to me, a little smile playing about his lips all the while. He gave the impression of being a good-natured fellow who was a bit drunk (he was drinking whiskey, with cheese to accompany it) and felt like chatting with someone. There was something amiable and appealing in his eyes. Normally, I would have begun a conversation from my side; but that evening I hadn't had much to drink, and besides, he was older than I was, around forty, and I didn't want to intrude. Despite being probably an affable sort of person, he also seemed shy, and somewhat feminine in manner. When he looked in my direction and smiled, it was in a guarded way, and for the most part he sat at an angle to me, showing his profile. He seemed hesitant and fidgety as he rested his chin on the flat handle of the walking stick that stood between his legs. And so there was no chance for us to speak until I was having my after-dinner cup of tea, when suddenly he made up his mind to address me.

"Excuse me, but aren't you Nakada Susumu, the movie director?"

I looked up again but had no recollection of his face or features, there between the upturned collar of his rain-spattered coat and the Taiwanese panama hat he wore on his head.

"Yes, I am. Forgive me if I've forgotten, but have we met somewhere?"

"No, tonight's the first time. You were at the Miyako Cinema a while ago, weren't you? I was sitting just behind you and your friends, and I could tell from your conversation that you were Mr. Nakada."

"Oh, so you saw the film, did you?"

"Yes, I did. I've seen just about every film that Fukamachi Yurako has been in."

"That's wonderful! I'm very grateful." It was, after all, not some high-school student talking, but a discriminating, fashionable gentleman, so I really was rather pleased.

"No, no, it embarrasses me to hear you say that. *I'm* the one who's grateful!" He drained the last drops of whiskey and set the glass down smartly on the marble tabletop, then turned, with his chin still propped on the cane handle, and drew his face closer to mine. "It may sound like flattery, but I really feel that yours are the only Japanese films worth seeing. Most Japanese directors are too tied to stupid sentimentalism. Plays and films both, they're mostly sob stories, but your films are really lively and a pleasure to watch. And that's the way films *ought* to be, after all. When I see one of your movies, Japan seems like a brighter place; it genuinely makes me feel good."

"I wish everyone felt that way, but there are people who say I'm just copying Hollywood."

"Well, who cares if it is copying Hollywood, as long as the films are entertaining! Of course if it was a bad imitation, it'd be another story; but you, you're making movies with exactly the same sensibility and ideals as American directors. Why, if the Americans saw them, they wouldn't find anything to complain about. How about it—have you ever shown any of your films to a Western audience?"

"No, of course not. I don't have that much confidence yet. . . ."

"Then you're being too modest. I've been seeing more of your movies than foreign ones lately, and I think they're every bit as good —in some cases, a lot better."

"Now that really *is* flattery!" I didn't know what his motive was, but he praised my films so much I felt disconcerted. Still, he didn't seem to be trying to make fun of me. I realized, though, that he was much drunker than he'd at first appeared to be. He had that heavy look about him which serious drinkers often have, his gaze rather fixed, his manner of speaking oddly calm, his face pale. So at first glance, apart from the moments when he gave me a sudden hard stare, he seemed quite normal, his words emerging with an almost annoying slowness in that flat tone of his.

"No, really, I'm serious," he said quietly. "Only, I wouldn't give you all the credit. No matter how good a director is, he has to have the right actor, and I think you've been very fortunate there. Fuka-michi Yurako is just right for a director of your tastes. It's as if she'd been born here just to appear in your movies. Without an actress like her, I don't think you'd be able to create the kind of world you're aiming at.... Oh, waitress! Bring us two whiskeys," he ordered in that quiet voice.

"I don't want one, thank you," I said.

"Oh, come on, join me in a drink. I want to drink to your films, and to the health of both you and Yurako."

Just what kind of work did this man do, I wondered. A news-paperman, perhaps? A lawyer? A senior bank official, leading a life of leisure? For, although at first he'd seemed timid, as he talked he began to relax and be more easygoing, treating me a bit as if I were a child. And he, being considerably older than me, seemed rather like a good-natured uncle to me; so, while not really wanting a drink, I decided not to resist.

"By the way, who wrote the original of your *A Woman Who Loves Black Cats*?"

"I did it myself, with the movie in mind. I always have to write in such a hurry that the result's never up to much...."

"No, it's a fine piece of work, and perfect for Yurako. There's that scene where she's taking a bath, and the cat jumps right in with her—how did you manage to train it so well?"

"It's our cat, and it's not shy at all with her."

"Really?... Well, they use animals a lot in foreign films, but it's rare in Japan. And Yurako was wonderful, as always. In the scene where she gets out of the bath, she appeared more or less half-naked. I'll bet she's the only actress here who could appear in a shot like that. Yes, that was a very daring shot," he said, nodding to himself.

"We had a lot of trouble with the censors over it. They're always on the lookout for something in my films, and this time they said it was more suggestive than anything in foreign films."

"That may well be," he said, laughing. "You know that part where she comes into the bedroom from the bath, and she's wearing this thin silk dressing gown, with the backlighting. . . ."

"Oh yes, that. They cut out two or three feet right there."

"Well, you can see her whole body through the gown. But that's not the first time you've done a shot like that, is it? I'm sure there was something just as daring in an earlier movie. . . . Wasn't it in *The Dream Dancer*?"

"Oh, you saw that too, did you?"

"Yes, I did. And there was a scene just like the one we've been talking about. Only, it wasn't in the bath. Yurako's playing a dancer, and she's changing costumes backstage. She wasn't wearing a stitch except around her breasts and hips, was she? And you didn't use backlighting for that scene, you used strong lighting from the side, so the light went from her right shoulder straight down, flowing along the surface of her leg down to the heels of her shoes."

"What an amazing memory you've got!" I said with some sincerity.

"Yes, well, I have my reasons for remembering that bit." He gave a self-satisfied little smile and leaned further toward me over the table. "It seems to me that there were two parts of her body shown in that film that had never appeared in any of your earlier works. You remember? You showed her navel in that film for the first time. Of course, I'd seen the section from just below her breasts down to her solar plexus before, in *Wild Young Thing*; but her navel was unknown territory. I'm *very* glad you did that. . . ."

Yurako, I remember perfectly well showing your navel in *The Dream Dancer*—I don't need anyone to remind me. I'm sure you haven't forgotten either. I've never filmed even the tiniest part of your body without a conscious motive. Even a single wrinkle resulting from a twist of some muscle never appeared by chance in any film of mine; it was all carefully planned beforehand. Just how many wrinkles would appear just where if you twisted your body in a certain direction, at a certain angle, and what kind of pattern of lines they would form—I thought of everything, as if I were dealing with the complexities of a plot. So I know he was right about both *The Dream Dancer* and *Wild Young Thing*, and it was gratifying to have him so alert to my intentions. But still, I couldn't help feeling that there was something skewed about his whole approach. He, on the other hand, seemed completely blind to any signs of strain on my face and just kept on talking, showing off his detailed knowledge of your body with real gusto.

"But, you know, I'd actually known for some time that her navel goes in—I can't stand protruding navels! Remember that scene in *Love on a Summer Night* when she comes out of the sea with her wet swimsuit stuck to her body? Well, you can just make out the indentation of her navel there. I'll bet you made her wear that wet swimsuit and went in for a close-up on purpose, just to show that little indentation, now didn't you? What a cunning director, I thought to myself —a regular von Stroheim! Anyway, in *Love on a Summer Night* it was *through* the clothing, but in *The Dream Dancer* there was nothing hiding it—it was *exactly* the kind of navel I'd imagined!"

"So, you're that keen on navels, then, are you?" I said in an attempt at sarcasm, but the fellow went on, as straight-faced as before.

"Not just navels, I'm keen on every part. There was another one I got to see for the first time in *The Dream Dancer*."

"Where?"

"Where? You must know where."

"But I don't. Was there another part like that?"

"There was indeed—the soles of her feet."

Seeing my startled look, he let out a burst of laughter.

"How about it—I'm right, aren't I? Yurako is dancing in her bare feet, and she steps on some bits of broken glass on the stage. The sweet girl then keeps on dancing, despite her pain. A little blood comes out of the soles of her feet, and her toeprints are left on the stage. The prints of the five toes on each foot are a bit spread apart, as if she were walking on tiptoe. That's right, I had a good look at her toeprints, especially the big toes!... Let's see, what happens next? Oh yes, after she dances, she goes all weak and falls down on the stage. Then an actor who's supposed to be in love with her picks her up and takes her backstage. He lines up two chairs and puts Yurako on them, and then he picks out the bits of glass from her feet and washes them. In order to examine the wounds properly, the actor has taken a table lamp and placed it on the floor so it lights up the soles of her feet from below. And it was then, you see, that I got a really good look at them for the first time...."

"I see—you're really just interested in seeing those parts, is that it?"

"Yes, you could say that. Aren't *you* aiming at that kind of audience response yourself? I would imagine that it's precisely someone like me you want in the audience, someone who watches your films with the same kind of sensibility as yours, who observes your film star's body as carefully as I do."

"Well, you may be right about that; but, you know, you do strike me as a little weird."

I noticed a malevolent, mad sort of light come into his drunken eyes. His face had grown paler and even his lips were dry and lusterless. I felt a vague premonition of disaster, but I couldn't run away —I was almost spellbound, somehow. I was also prey to a kind of curiosity, naturally enough.

"What do you mean by that—'weird'?"

"Yes, well, let's discuss that later."

He called the waitress over again, shouting "Two more whiskeys!" then continued: "You think you know more about her body than anyone else in the world, presumably."

"Yes, of course I do. I've directed her for years now; and, besides, as perhaps you're aware, she is my wife."

"You are indeed married to her. Now, what I'd like to do is try to determine which of us—you, her husband, or myself—is better versed in the geography of her body. No doubt you'll think me a bit 'weird' for making such an odd suggestion. But you have before you some-one who's never actually met your wife. Now let us suppose that this person has spent a long time researching, on the basis of films alone, all the various parts of your wife's body, going five or six times to see certain close-up scenes so as to ascertain just what her shoulders are like, and her breasts, and her buttocks; and that by now he has such a firm grasp of it all that even when he closes his eyes, he can picture certain details exactly, Then, one evening, the man happens to meet the woman's husband, to meet the person who, it may be as-sumed, has ✳✳✳✳✳✳ her. In this case, surely, the 'odd suggestion' would really be quite natural."

"Hmmm. And I take it that you are that man, and you have such knowledge of my wife's body. Is that right?"

"Yes, definitely. If you think I'm lying, try asking me about it, any-thing you like."

As I sat there, silent and blinking uncertainly, he went on relent-lessly: "Take for example her shoulders: they're fleshy, and slope gently downward. Partly because of the long nape of the neck, the line from the base of the ear to the top of the arm joint is so smooth that, viewed from the side, it's hard to tell where the arm begins. The neck is surrounded by thick fatty tissue, so that the bones and muscles of the throat are barely visible. Only when she turns her head a little can you see the bone behind the ear protruding slightly. Now, to move on to the back: the shoulder blades are concealed by fatty tissue when the arms are allowed to hang down in a natural way; but that doesn't mean that the dividing line between them is completely undetectable. The reason is that Yurako's backbone is deeply recessed all the way down, making her back look as if it were two separate cylinders joined together. The gap between the two cylinders is her backbone. That furrow is always dark, unless a strong light is shone directly on the back. When she stands up straight, the high curves of her buttocks near the bottom of the backbone and around the joints of the hips make the furrow all the more pronounced. When she twists her body to the left, two thick creases appear on the side she's twisted toward. The flesh between those two lines rises up to form a little mound. At the same time, on her right side, you catch a glimpse of the bottommost curve of her ribs. . . ."

What a creep, I thought to myself; but all the while the lovely shape of your back rose vividly before my mind's eye. And as you read this, I can imagine you perhaps wanting to strip naked and stand in front of a mirror. I can see you checking the deep furrow of your backbone, and the two creases on your side, and the exposed lowest rib. I can imagine you thinking about how very closely this man has observed you in your films, and feeling somehow as unnerved as I did.

"Yes, yes, you've got it absolutely right. And what about parts other than her back?" I couldn't help asking, finding myself drawn in against my will.

"Do you have a pencil?" he said, opening the paper menu on the table. "Let me explain this to you with a drawing—it's tiresome to do it in words." Then he began to draw, in order: your arms, like so; your hands, thus; your thighs, like this; your neck, like that. In the way he drew the lines, there was nothing of the skill you'd expect from an artist. (And my hunch that he wasn't one was confirmed later.) "This part here is like *this*, and here is like . . . *that*. . .," he said, drawing the awkward lines very slowly, as if he were tracing them. Sometimes he'd close his eyes and look upward, apparently trying to get the picture in his brain in perfect focus. But in those clumsy sketches and childish diagrams that gradually emerged from the faltering pencil strokes, there was a certain form which tenaciously counterfeited the reality, with a queer profusion of detail and a crudity that only an amateur would be capable of. If it were just a matter of skillfully capturing certain characteristics and drawing a kind of cartoonist's likeness so that one could tell whose face it was, there'd be nothing very difficult in that. But it wasn't the face he was drawing. He drew your arms, your fingers, your thighs, all in separate fragments, and in such a way that, to my eyes, they could only have belonged to you. He knew every dimple and every wrinkle in your body. One probably couldn't call it art, but it certainly showed an astonishing memory! And he assembled all those remembered parts and, without leaving one out, carefully put them down on paper.

Later, I was often reminded of the sketches he drew that evening whenever I passed in front of Arita's Drugstore: the clammy, faintly gruesome look of those waxen hands and heads in there . . . and yet with, somehow, the look of real human skin. . . . That's exactly what this man's sketches were like. When, for example, he drew the area from your thighs to your knees, he'd do it twice, distinguishing between when you had your legs stretched out and when you had them bent, and how much of a change that made in the dimples on your knees, and what bits of you looked firmer and what looked more slack, as a result. He'd sketch in shadows with very fine lines to show where you bulge out, and I must say he was clever at capturing the way the flesh is distributed over your body. Merely by drawing the line from your rounded heel to your arch, he could suggest your whole foot. And he didn't overlook the fact that your second toes are longer than your big toes, and that they usually overlap the big toes a bit. When he drew the soles of your feet, he copied the pads of all five toes on each foot, getting the special features of each—the pad of the little toe being different from that of the third toe, and so on. If I hadn't had the experience of helping you polish your toenails, I would never have been able to make such fine distinctions myself, and would have been badly put to shame by him.

"Finding out what her breasts and buttocks looked like—now that really took an effort!" the man confessed. According to him, there's hardly any part of your body that hasn't by now been exposed on film; only the areas of your breasts, hips, and buttocks have always been covered by a single layer of cloth. For a long time he'd been paying close attention to the bumps and cavities visible through that cloth. Then, fortunately, you appeared in *The Dream Dancer* in a single chemise, and at one point the strings of the garment came loose. Just then, you bent forward to pick up a rose that had fallen to the floor. The chemise naturally sagged open a bit; and from between the loosened strings, he could glimpse your breasts—to use his words, "as round as the breasts of an Indian virgin," like "two great swellings" rooted in your chest. He couldn't actually see your nipples, but he saw enough to imagine the whole shape. If someone can get to know all but one or two particular parts of a person's body, it should be possible to accurately construe those missing parts, just as one can move from known quantities to an unknown quantity in an algebraic equation. Thus he claimed to have deduced, by assembling the known fragments of your body from various cinematic scenes, the bits that were unknown—the "sun and shade" of your buttock muscles, for example. . . .

"You see? I can draw a map of her body showing the location of each and every hill and valley, as precise and detailed as any map made by the General Ordnance Survey. You claim to be her husband, but I wonder if you've memorized her body in quite such detail."

The tabletop was by now littered with scraps of paper. After he'd drawn his "map" all over the back of the menu, he extracted from his pocket a program from the Miyako Cinema and used the back of that to sketch on. Then he used some paper napkins and finally the marble tabletop itself. This task appeared to produce in him an extreme of pleasure and excitement; it looked as if he would go on forever, if left to himself.

"I'm sorry," I had to tell him, "but I get the point. You've shown me quite enough. I'm just no match for you!"

"And . . . let's see . . . yes! When she's doing an action film and has to show violent emotion, she sometimes pants heavily, right? Then the bone at the base of her neck, right here, sticks out just a trifle from the fatty tissue—like this. . . ."

"No, really, that's enough! Please, let's leave it right there!"

"Ah-ha-ha-ha! But why? I'm just drawing you a nude portrait of the woman you love!"

"Yes, I know, and it makes me feel uncomfortable."

"*Now* listen to you! Aren't you always making movies with your wife virtually naked in them? Isn't that how you make your living? I'm the one who's at a disadvantage here. It took a huge effort to get to the point of being able to draw pictures like this!"

"All right, all right. I'll just take these sketches home with me, then, and show them to my wife." With that, I stuffed the scraps of paper into my pocket. Whether because he secretly hoped I'd show them to you, or because he didn't care about those particular drawings since he could always draw more, he let me do as I wished. Naturally, I had no intention of showing you anything, and later I tore them up and threw them in the toilet. If I *had* shown them to you, I'm sure you would have been disgusted. Just imagine your lovely body being turned into the wax models that are on display at Arita's Drugstore. . . .

"Well, if you're leaving, I'll go part of the way with you," said the man, so we left the café together sometime around nine o'clock. I had already spent close to two hours drinking with this person about whom I knew almost nothing, so why did I agree to spend more time with him? I suppose it was because, though he seemed a bit sinister, I'd also begun to have a certain fellow feeling toward him. If I found him "weird," wasn't it because there were aspects of him that were all too much like myself? He was staring at every nook and cranny of your body with the same eye as I did. Moreover, he hadn't actually met you in person even once. He had just suddenly popped up like a genie and started discoursing on the beauty of someone —the love of my life—whom no one but me should have known in such detail. I had no reason to be jealous of him, because all he knew was an illusion in a film, not you yourself, my wife. Why shouldn't a man who loves a shadow and a man who loves the reality shake hands together, just as the shadow and the reality are amiably bound up with one another?

These were my thoughts as I followed him. He turned off Kyō-goku toward Kawaramachi and began walking along the dimly lit street. Through the clouds in the sky above, here and there one could see stars faintly shining, then disappearing. The whole area was still shrouded in a misty drizzle, and his form, hazily illuminated by streetlamps from time to time, seemed itself like a kind of "shadow."

"I suppose you think, of course, that she belongs to no one else but you. . . ," he said as if half to himself. "But how would you feel if I told you that, at the same time she's your wife, she's also mine?"

"No problem at all. Go ahead, be married to her. I hope you'll be very, very good to her." I tried to make a joke of it.

"You mean, the one who's *my* wife would just be a film clip, so you wouldn't need to feel any concern or jealousy—that's what you think, and it makes you feel easier, correct?"

"Well, if I allowed myself to worry about things like that, I wouldn't be able to survive as an actress's husband for a single day."

"Yes, I see what you mean. But think again a little more carefully. Let me ask you this: first, which of us do you think is Yurako's real husband, and which do you think experiences the greater happiness and pleasure as a husband?"

"That's a tough question." There was nothing I could do but shrug it off as a joke. Still, the fellow peered at me through the darkness and gazed pityingly into my face.

"This is no joke, you know—I'm talking seriously. Unless I'm mistaken, you're thinking along these lines: the person *he* loves is a shadow, while the one *I* love is a reality. So there can in fact be no problem. But won't you admit that, to you too, the woman who appears in the film is not some dead object but a living being?"

"Yes, I admit that. It's as you say."

"Well then, at least one can't claim that the Yurako on film is just a shadow of the Yurako who is your wife, since the one on film is alive too. Let's not forget this, it's important: your wife may be a reality, but the one on film is an independent reality as well. Now, you might want to say that this is all just sophistry. Given that there are two realities, which of them first came into the world? If your wife did not exist, there could be no Yurako on film. The one depends on the other. But then I would ask: where, except on film, does the truly beautiful woman you love, I daresay even adore, exist? At home, does she strike the alluring poses we see in *The Dream Dancer*, *A Woman Who Loves Black Cats*, and *Wild Young Thing*? In which sphere does her life as a woman exist?..."

"You're right. I sometimes feel the same way myself. I call it my 'philosophy of film-making.' "

"Oh, I see—your 'philosophy of film-making,' is it?" he said in a curiously aggressive manner. "Well, then, couldn't we perhaps put it like this: the Yurako on film is the reality, while your wife is just her shadow? How would that accord with your philosophy? Your wife will gradually grow older, but the woman on film will remain young and beautiful, frisking about in all her glorious vitality, forever. Let's imagine you ten years from now, tenderly visualizing her as she was before, thinking to yourself, *Oh, she wasn't like this back then. Where did those wrinkles come from? She never had them there before! And those charming little hollows at every joint of her body—where have they gone?* Then let's suppose you take out the old reels and put them on the projector. You'll discover that those little hollows have not disappeared, or gone anywhere at all; they're there on her body, forever. Your wife may have aged, but the dream dancer still conceals her rounded breasts under her chemise, and picks up the rose that's fallen on the floor. The woman who loves black cats is still in her bath, splashing the water as she plays with her cat. Then you'll realize that your young and beautiful wife has fled into the film, and the woman who's there beside you now is just her shell. You'll stare at those movies in puzzlement and think: were these films *I* made? Could such a radiant world have come from us, my wife and me? And in the end you'll recognize that the films are not things you two alone created; that the dancer and the wild thing were not the products of your direction and your wife's acting skills but had been there, living within the film, from the very beginning. They represent an 'eternal woman,' quite different from your wife. Your wife became the vehicle for her—that's all—the image of that feminine spirit for a while. You both are just making a living out of her, the eternal woman. I'm sure you'll come to realize that. . . ."

"Yes, well, that's a very interesting theory. But, you know, just as my wife will grow old, so too the woman in the film will become dim and fuzzy as time goes by. Film itself isn't an eternal, unchanging medium. . . ."

"All right. But I have something to say on that point, too. Do you know why I go so often to see Yurako's movies? And why I've memorized the geography of her body in such detail? As I showed you earlier with the drawings, I can gaze at her body as I like, even with my eyes shut. If I say 'Come on, Yurako, stand up!' she stands. If I say 'Sit down, please' or 'Lie down, please,' she does what I ask. I can strip her naked and stare at her back, her buttocks, anywhere I like. Or I can turn her upside down and have a good look at the soles of her feet. You say you're her husband, but can you handle your wife as freely as that? And even if you can, could you embrace her right now, as we walk? *My* Yurako comes whenever I call and never pouts, no matter how demanding I might be. *Your* wife will get old; but mine, even if the film itself does fade, will always be alive here in my mind. In other words, the real Yurako—her essence, if you like—lives in my brain. The one on film is a ghost of her; and your wife is a ghost of that, at one more remove!"

"But, as you said yourself a few moments ago, without my wife, there would be no film. And without the film, the woman in your mind wouldn't exist either, would she? Besides, when you die, what becomes of that eternal 'essence'? It seems to me your theory breaks down there."

"Not at all. Before you or I came into the world, there existed an unchanging essence which we might as well call 'the Yurako type.' It manifests itself in various ways, now appearing on film, now as a living person. For instance, I used to like the films with Marie Prevost, the American, in them. I bet you like them too. No, never mind, there's no need even to ask," he said, taking in the surprised look on my face. "Now when you discovered your wife, I'm quite sure you thought to yourself here was a Japanese version of Marie Prevost.

And wasn't there—yes, of course there was!—a scene where Prevost is taking a bath, too? In just the same way as Yurako, she comes out of the bathroom wearing a flimsy gown and puts on her slippers there in the doorway.... How many years ago was that? It's a very old movie, but I still remember it well. Prevost is standing with her back to us, in a sexy pose, and steps into her slippers. As she does so, she shows us the soles of her feet. Am I right? You remember it too, don't you? They shot that scene in soft focus so you could see her body only vaguely, but the impression of her face and physique was just like your wife's, don't you think? Especially in the close-ups, you could see how the line of her nostrils when she was looking up was just like Yurako's. And the dimples on her arms and hands were in just the same places. I'm sure there'd be lots more points in common if you could see her naked, and I have the feeling that her navel is recessed.... Unfortunately I don't actually know for sure. The only ones I'm quite certain about are Yurako's and Pola Negri's in *Sumu-run*.... Anyway, it's not only Prevost, there are a good many women in the world who resemble your wife. If you don't believe me, let me ask you if you've ever bought the favors of F...ko in the X House in the Shizuoka red-light district. Of course she's not as good-looking as Prevost or your wife; she doesn't quite come up to scratch. But even so, she's certainly the 'Yurako type.' The dimples you find all over her body are similar, and her breasts in particular are *exactly* like hers. Then, there's ****** and ******."

Thus he went on totting up all the "Yurako types" he knew. They might not be exactly like you in every physical respect, but they had the same feel to their skin, the same general aura; and they all had one part that was exactly like you. For example, as he mentioned, F...ko of Shizuoka has the same breasts. Your shoulders are apparently to be found on K...ko, a prostitute in Tokyo's Asakusa. S...ko from the O House in the Nagano red-light area has your buttocks. A certain girl in Hōjō, Chiba, has your knees, while your neck is in the possession of someone at the Beppu hot springs in Kyushu. In the same way, your hands are to be found in such-and-such a place, your thighs somewhere else. He had carried on his research into the various parts of your body not only through the movies but also through these women. As he said, the "map" he spoke of earlier is a "map" of them, as well as a "map" of you.

"And you know, you're in luck! That lovely backbone of hers is right nearby! You know the Tobita quarters in Osaka? Well, just go there, ask for A...ko at the B House, and have her show you her back. And even closer by, in Goban-chō here in Kyoto, you'll find her feet. It's a girl called D...ko at the C House. On Japanese feet the second toe is almost never longer than the big toe, but hers is an exact match!..."

Then he started expounding his theory of "essence," lining up difficult names like Plato and Weininger, but I neither remember all his tedious arguments nor have the energy to record them here. The point seems to be that you, "Yurako," have dwelt in the "Mind of the Universe" from the beginning. God, following that eternal pattern, creates women of a certain type and sends them into this world. He further creates men who see a special kind of beauty only in those particular women. My drinking companion and I are members of that male group in whose minds and hearts you also dwell, apparently. Since this world of ours is itself an illusion, the human you and the you on film are, likewise, illusions. However, the filmed illusion lasts longer than the human one, and captures the various forms of the woman when she is at her youngest and loveliest. For that reason, of all the things on this earth, this is the closest to the "essence." It is, he claims, something that comes about at one stage in the process of returning the human illusion to the "Mind of the Universe"....

"So when you look at it this way, what difference really is there between us, as her partners in life? Is there even one kind of happi-

ness you have that I don't? I know her body as well as you do, or
even better! I can call her to my side anywhere, in any circumstances,
strip off her kimono, have her lie down, get up.... And that's not all:
I can ****** her. But even that's not everything, either. As the perfect
'Yurako,' she ******, too.... All right then, come with me—I'll show
you where I live. The fact is I've got my own 'Yurako' at home."

I couldn't help standing stock still for a moment and gazing into
his face.

"What? You've got a Yurako too? Are you talking about your wife?"

"Yes, my wife. And which of them, my wife or yours, is closer to
the real 'Yurako,' I'll be happy to demonstrate, if you like."

It goes without saying that my curiosity had reached its peak by
this time. The man's words and actions were more and more surprising. There certainly are some very strange people in the world. Still,
some of the things he said hit the mark and seemed consistent with
what I felt, so I was fairly sure he wasn't mad. Or, even if he was a
bit crazy, I had to admire the precision of his observations of the
opposite sex and the subtlety of his reactions. Naturally I was more
than eager to meet his wife—the woman he called "Yurako." Then
too, he hadn't yet told me who he really was, and by now I was very
curious to know that as well.

"So how about it? Wouldn't you like to see her for yourself?" he
said, casting a sidelong glance at my face, and giving his question a
strangely unpleasant weight.

"How can I resist? I absolutely must meet her."

"Will you come to my house, then?"

"Yes, of course. When should I come?"

"Anytime. Tonight would be fine."

"Tonight?"

"Yes, why not now?"

"But it's so late. Where in fact do you live?"

"Right close by."

"What do you mean by 'close'?"

"Why, a mere five or ten minutes from here by car."

Looking around, I realized we'd come as far as the neighborhood of the Demachi Bridge. The time was around ten-thirty. The man was casually suggesting that I "come tonight," but did he really mean to take this relative stranger home with him at this late hour and introduce him to his wife? Was he so proud of her as to insist on doing this?

"It seems a bit crazy. Am I being 'taken for a ride'?"

"Ah-ha-ha-ha! Do I look like a crook?"

"But it'll be eleven by the time we get there. It may be all right with you, but what about your wife?"

"Ah, but she's a very accommodating person. She never gets angry with me, however late it is. She's always there with a welcoming smile on her face. We're the most loving couple in the world—as I hope to show you soon."

"Don't be silly, I'd be much too embarrassed!"

"Yes, well, it's not a bad thing, perhaps, that you should expect to be embarrassed."

"Why?"

"Maybe you're too easily embarrassed."

"Maybe, a little—I don't know what to say."

"Ah-ha-ha-ha. You're always showing off *your* wife in public, so tonight it's your turn to see *mine*. It'd be cowardly to run away now. So come along—come on." Even as he said this, he was taking my arm and pulling me toward the taxi stand at the west end of the nearby bridge.

"Don't worry, I'm not going to run away," I assured him.

Leaving me to wait in front of the taxi office, he strode in on his own and told the man our destination in a low voice. And now for the first time since leaving the café, I had a chance to see him in the light. The liquor he'd been drinking seemed to be having its effect: he had at some point turned into a different person. His eyes now had a wild and wanton gleam to them, his mouth was slack, his nostrils wide with excitement. The old Taiwanese panama which he'd had pulled down over his eyes had shifted so it sat on the back of his head, making him look like a spoiled kid. With the crinkly hair that spilled messily down over his forehead, the impression he gave was of an aging delinquent. As for his actual age: I had earlier guessed him to be about forty years old, but now, with his hat pushed back, I could see a surprising number of fine wrinkles on his face, while the skin around his eyes was slack. His hair was dull and lusterless, and his sideburns had turned partly white. He must have been at least forty-seven or -eight—an old man!—almost fifty. I could tell from his droopy manner and unsure way of walking that he was far drunker than I'd imagined. Yet he seemed not to have reached his limit; once inside the car, he kept shouting at the driver hoarsely, "Hey, aren't we there yet?" and taking a swig from a strange-looking container of a sort I'd never seen before. It was a thin, flat object, like a silver cigarette case.

"What's that?"

"This? It's something Americans use to carry liquor in, on the sly. You must've seen it in the movies."

"Oh, that! And they're selling them in Japan now, too?"

"I bought it when I was over there. It's very handy for taking the occasional nip. . . ."

"No stopping you, is there? Do you always carry it around with you?"

"Oh, only at night. My wife is a funny one—she's all in favor of my coming home dead-drunk in the early hours."

"So your wife drinks too?"

"No, she doesn't, but she likes to see me drunk. In other words—

how shall I put it?—she waits till I'm blotto, and then comes on to me in the craziest way."

This sent chills up and down my spine. He kept on laughing as he described their lovemaking in distasteful detail, looking into my eyes mockingly as he did so. My face must have turned dead-white. What a creepy old lecher he was! Perhaps he was, after all, half-cracked? And he kept going on about this lovely young wife of his, but was an old coot like this likely to have one? Maybe it was just a mistress he had tucked away somewhere.

Very soon, the taxi with the two of us in the back was jolting along over an extremely dark, badly paved road. I had only been in Kyoto for a few months at that point, so I can't be sure exactly where we passed through that night; but soon after we crossed the Demachi Bridge, the Kamo River was no longer visible. We drove along streets barely wide enough to let us through, as if pushing our way between the rows of houses crowding on either side, turning now right, now left. The rain had stopped, but since the sky was still thickly clouded over, we could see no trace of the mountains. With all the houses' doors and shutters closed, it was impossible to tell what sort of neighborhood it was, but here and there I could hear the sound of water rushing through a channel, as from some mountain stream. The man stuck his head out the window occasionally and gave directions to the driver: "Turn there . . . this way. . . ." Gradually the houses grew fewer, and paddies and trees appeared, with thick clumps of grass— clearly we were now on a country road on the outskirts of the city.

"Where is this? Where are we going? It seems awfully far."

"Don't worry. We're being driven there, so just keep quiet and leave everything to me. You're in my hands tonight. All right? Do you agree?"

"But, really, is this right, coming all this way out?"

"Right? Of course it is. I'm not too drunk to know where my own house is, you know. . . . How about a swig?"

Every time the taxi swayed, he lurched heavily into me; and all the while, he was taking swigs from the flask he held with one shaking hand. After offering me a drink, he began to nuzzle insistently at my neck, as if I were a woman he had designs on. His reeking breath and the greasy feel of his hands on me were disgusting. This was obviously a man who couldn't hold his liquor, the type who made a habit of annoying other people when drunk. What a mess I'd got myself into!

"Look, I'm sorry, but could you take your hand away from there? You're squeezing far too hard."

"Ah-ha-ha-ha! Too much for you, is it?"

"Yes, way too much!"

"Shall I give you a little kiss?"

"You m-must be j-joking. . . ."

"Ah-ha-ha-ha! How many times a day do you kiss your Yurako? Oh, come on, you can tell *me*! Three? Four? Maybe . . . ten?"

"Well . . . how often do you do it?"

"Me? I can't count the times. Her face, her hands, between her fingers, the soles of her feet, everywhere! . . ." Suddenly he drooled a bit onto my cheek.

"Aagh! . . . Hey, could you please . . . move your face . . . the other way."

"Never mind, never mind. What would you do if it were her, not me? I bet you'd lap it up!"

"Just speak for yourself."

"I *am*—I'd suck it all right up, that's what I'd do."

"You're a fool, then!"

"Of course I am. Anyone's a fool when he's under a woman's thumb. 'All for love,' as the saying goes."

"Yes, but you don't have to *lick* her *dribble* up. . . . By the way, how old is she?"

"She's young! How old would you guess?"

"I wouldn't know.... Judging from your age—"

"I'm an old coot, but my wife's a lot younger. Why, she's as lively as an untamed filly. So, how old would you say?"

"Which is older, my wife or yours? Mine is just twenty."

"Then they're the same."

"As young as that?... Sorry, but is she by any chance your second wife?"

"She's my first wife, my main wife, my single prized possession—higher than a goddess to me." He gave a loud laugh and continued, drooling a bit as he did: "How about that? Impressed, aren't you? I come home alone every night around this time, traveling along this lonely road through the rice fields, to see her. I don't come by car, I walk.... And my wife listens for my footsteps, drowsing there behind the curtains in the bedroom, all soft and languid, curled up like a cat, her body perfumed, clean, and pretty.... I enter the bedroom quietly and gently part the curtains: 'Yurako, I'm home!' I say. 'You must've been *so* lonely.'"

"What?"

"Ah-ha-ha-ha! Are you surprised?"

"Do you mean to say her name is actually 'Yurako'?"

"Yes, that's what I call her—Yurako. Otherwise it just wouldn't feel right."

At last our car came to a stop at the foot of a thickly wooded hill.

"Here we are, here we are," he said, going ahead of me as he climbed the steep stone steps. I noted that he took out a flashlight to show the way, and realized he'd been telling the truth about coming home late like this every night. On either side of the steps grew a mass of yellow kerria flowers, so luxuriant that my trouser cuffs became entangled in them. The sultry smell of foliage filled my nostrils, and the flashlight's beam revealed now and then the bright green of spring leaves.

"There, there it is!" he said, and I looked toward the top of the slope to see a white-walled Western-style house with a single light shining over the door. It was too dark for me to see anything clearly, but the place stood by itself up there, with no other houses in sight. I sensed from the smells of earth and greenery and the general at-mosphere that the whole area was a grove or a small forest, and, judging from the gloomy shadows that covered what lay behind, I guessed it to be a cliff or mountainside. Right at the top of the steps was a recessed entranceway rather like an alcove cut into the white wall. I thought at first that the door was a wooden one, some three feet across; but on closer inspection it turned out to be glass. From a distance it had looked like a black wooden door because no lights were on inside the house. The single light I'd seen from the bottom of the steps was set over the recessed entrance and, protected by a cylindrical shade, it inscribed a vague circle of light on the white wall. I called the house "Western-style," but its outward appearance suggested a squarish bungalow, which would have been drab if seen by daylight. . . .

Panting, he drew from his pocket a rattling key chain and opened the door. I followed him into the entrance hall. He locked the door from the inside, slipped off his muddy shoes, and seemed to fumble about for his slippers. There must have been a light switch some-where, but he made no attempt to turn it on to aid his efforts. The light outside was hazily reflected through the glass door, but I could make nothing out in the entrance hall by its uncertain glow. Given that his panting breaths immediately filled the space with the smell of whiskey, it must been rather small; I felt as if I were boxed up inside four narrow walls. Then he turned on the flashlight again, directing its beam toward the floor, apparently searching for something. By the flickering, shifting light, I saw a large china jar for holding walking sticks and a hatstand with a mirror attached. There were three or four hats hanging there: a soft homburg, a gray derby, a hunting cap, and an ordinary straw hat. Beneath the hatstand were two or three pairs of slippers, one of which was a woman's, made of bright pink silk, with high heels in the French fashion. It was this that first caught me by surprise: the reason being that, though it had clearly seen much use, with the shiny outline of a footprint visible inside, still, had I been shown it somewhere without explanation, I would have assumed it was one of yours. It looked exactly like the pair in our house, so well worn by you. It had wrinkles in the same spots, the traces of your heel and toes were visible at the same points, it was soiled in just the same pattern. The moment I saw it, I recalled with utmost clarity the lovely shape of your feet. At any rate, those slippers had been worn by feet that were the same as yours. *What? Is my wife here?* I thought for a moment.

He carefully put the slippers to one side—I'm sure he must have wanted me to see them—and, picking up some leather ones, tossed them in front of me: "Wear these," he said. He turned off the flashlight and, walking ahead of me, proceeded straight down a dark corridor. Along this passageway, so narrow that we had no choice but to walk in single file, he half-stumbled, bumping against either wall as he went. It may have been partly that he was relaxed now that he'd returned to his own house, but we were both the worse for drink. At any rate, the night was as humid as if it had been the rainy season, so inside the house was like a steambath, on top of which his whiskey-breath filled the corridor, blowing in gusts into my face. I felt my neck grow hot, and the effects of the liquor spread throughout my body.

"Come right this way," he said, as we reached the end of the corridor, leading me into a room to the left. He lit a match and, holding up the flickering flame, advanced five or six steps into the room. There was a table there, and on it a candlestick. He transferred the flame he was holding to the candle.

As the candle's flame gradually grew, the thick darkness receded little by little from around the table. Still, I couldn't tell how large the room was or what it might contain. Then he and I sat down opposite each other with the candlestick between us. My gaze happened to fall on his face, glowing red in the ray of candlelight. What I was looking at, however, was not in fact his face but the crown of his head, in all its shining baldness. He had taken off his panama hat and placed it on the table. He looked exhausted as he sat slumped in the chair, his arms dangling down like a puppet whose strings have been cut; he was still panting heavily, his head bent forward, which was why what stared back at me wasn't his face but his bald pate. Even so, it took some time for my fuddled brain to take in the fact that it was a human head. After all, I hadn't dreamed until then that he could be so magnificently bald. Admittedly, there were a few messy locks of curly hair on his forehead and also at the back, making a kind of fringe, so that with his hat on, his baldness was nicely covered. I sat there stunned for a bit, staring at the bald patch, round as a bull's-eye. The man was not just "almost fifty"; he must have been several years older. . . .

Suddenly he stood up without a word, moved quickly to one corner of the room, and began to drink something, making great gurgling sounds. *Ah, you're having some water to sober up*, I thought at first, since he was drinking so greedily. But a closer look revealed that there was a shelf with five or six bottles of Western liquors in that corner. He was standing in front of it, helping himself. After downing five or six glasses without a pause, he came back toward me, licking his wet lips contentedly (they may have been wet with drool, for all I know). He stood there for a moment, then took the candlestick from the table.

"Now then, let's introduce you to my wife!"

"But, where is she?"

"In the room over there. Just follow me—quietly; she'll be sound asleep by now."

"She's sleeping? Well then, we mustn't—"

"It's all right, I tell you! Here's her bedroom, see?" Even as he spoke, the flame of the candle in his hand revealed the doorway to the next room. It was a very strange room indeed, more a spacious closet than a room, actually—that was how it looked by candlelight. It was separated from the other room by a dark reddish-brown curtain which opened like a stage curtain to reveal a space hung about on three sides by other curtains of the same color. In the middle was a large bed, which occupied almost the whole room. The bed itself was surrounded on all four sides by hanging drapery, like the curtained daises of ancient Japan. It was, in effect, a Chinese-style bed. The hangings seemed to be (I couldn't say for sure) of a dark green velvet-like material. These layers upon layers of dark-colored cloth reminded me strongly of the stage props of some professional magician, if you can imagine that.

"She's asleep in here. Now, what shall I begin by showing you? Shall we make it her back? Or her belly? Or her feet?..."

He stretched out a hand and, fumbling through the curtain, began to rub what appeared to be the body of his sleeping wife. His eyes were bloodshot, and he had a smirk on his lips.

Having written this much, I'm sure you know already what it was that was sleeping in that bed. I myself had guessed from his earlier comments that it might well be a doll. But what was really creepy was not only the fact that it was a perfect copy of you but also that he had any number of such dolls, which he referred to as "the Real Yurakos." There was one of you sleeping, and one of you standing, and one of you with your thighs open, and one of you twisting your torso—and every kind of lewd posture imaginable, such that I can't bring myself to describe them. I saw fifteen or sixteen of them, but according to him "There are as many as thirty Yurakos here."

I've often heard stories of how sailors have full-scale rubber dolls to relieve their boredom during long sea voyages; but I'd never actually seen such a thing, and I doubted whether in fact they really existed. But that's exactly what this fellow's dolls were. He had each of his thirty "wives" carefully folded up, wrapped in a *furoshiki* cloth, and placed on a shelf. There were any number of such shelves hidden behind the curtains that hung down on three sides of the bedroom— his "magician's props." Each shelf was labeled with some sort of coded letter. Imagine how odd he looked taking down one of the bundles from a shelf, bustling about like the head clerk at a draper's getting ready to show a customer a roll of cloth. "Well now," he'd say, "what shall I show you next? My wife in a squatting posture?" And imagine those fifteen or sixteen figures of you, life-sized, silently lined up, standing there in that dead-quiet room near midnight. And then imagine the accustomed skill with which he inflated the flattened, folded dolls. When he turned on a tap and lit the gas, he got hot water right away (the workings were obscured by the curtains); a pipe led the hot water to a hole in the doll's body, which swelled up as we watched, gradually assuming a human shape; and as bit by bit partic-ular indentations and extrusions became visible, what emerged from the arms, the shoulders, the back, the legs was, unmistakably, you.

Almost ludicrous care had been taken regarding the design and placement of the hole through which the water was introduced. There was no sign of an unsightly stopper, as on an ice-pack, for example. With each and every doll, the **** was a work of art, though I won't insult you by going into any detail. I also assume he took considerable pleasure in the act of inserting the hosepipe. "I'm performing a work of creation, like God himself!" he claimed. "I don't know just how the God of old blew his breath into Adam and Eve when he created them, but I'm sure it must have been an interesting exercise."

You're probably thinking that, however lifelike I may say they were, they couldn't really amount to much since they were just dolls made of rubber. It must all sound silly to you. It's only natural for you to feel that way, not having seen or heard the evidence of the extraordinary pains he took to sew together those amazingly detailed pouches. I myself, having had it explained to me how he went about it, would be quite incapable of doing it myself, even if asked to try. Needless to say, he did everything himself, from buying the materials to adding the finishing touches. If you ever saw his workshop, you'd know that was the case. You'd discover that he had collected, with appalling diligence and persistence, every scrap of information he could possibly get about your body. If a person were shut up in a room lined with mirrors on every surface, he'd go mad, they say; and that's exactly the feeling *you* would experience in this man's little factory.

"Come have a look at this room over here," he said, leading me to the workshop, which was on the opposite side of the corridor. What met my eyes there was an assortment of fragments of limbs lined up on the floor, the walls, the ceiling, in every available space. Strangest of all were the photographs pasted everywhere—greatly enlarged photos of each part of your body, including your most private parts, and the details of single muscles. Now at last I understood how he was able to draw those uncanny sketches, so reminiscent of the wax figures at Arita's Drugstore, given that he spent his days gazing at this amazing collection of photographs. But even so, how had he got hold of them? How had he taken these photos, never having met you? In response to my questions, he brought out some scraps of old film, cut from a variety of motion pictures. The short ones consisted of one or two shots, the long ones of ten to twenty. He'd assembled every scene that was necessary to him from all of your movies. The dream dancer bending to pick up a rose on the floor and dancing on the stage with feet that drip blood, with a blowup of the bloody prints of her toes; the scene where the area from below the breasts to the solar plexus is clearly shown, from *Wild Young Thing*; the recessed navel from *Love on a Summer Night*—virtually all the scenes that he'd earlier displayed such elaborate knowledge of were there. He told me that he'd gone once to Okayama in the west and again to Utsunomiya in the east, from theater to theater, in pursuit of a certain movie: he wanted to obtain just one small segment of film in which he could clearly see the shape of your ears and how your teeth were set in your mouth.

". . . And that's when I discovered that there are lots of eccentric fellows just like me in the world. Let me explain. Say a certain film of Yurako's is first released in Tokyo and Kansai, and then is gradually distributed to the smaller cities in the provinces. In the process, the film gets shorter and shorter, oddly enough. Of course, there may be cases where the local censor decides to cut a particular scene. But since the censorship standards are pretty much the same from prefecture to prefecture, there shouldn't be too many different cuts. Strange, then, isn't it, that a scene that starts out by having twenty frames is reduced to fifteen, or ten, or, in extreme cases, none at all as it travels from city to city? It's because somebody is cutting out certain frames along the way! There are people out there waiting for Yurako to come along so they can tear off a hand or a foot, like starving wolves. If you want proof that there are lots of men like that, just try asking a projectionist in a country town somewhere. They're wise to the situation, and if you give them a little money, they'll clip out a shot or two to sell you on the sly. Why, it's regarded as one of the perks of the job!"

His labors were like those of a paleontologist. Just as the paleontologist unearths bones from age-old layers of soil and reconstructs the forms of animals that lived tens of thousands of years ago, this man collects your scattered limbs from all over the country, and tries to put together a perfect "you." The large photographs pasted to the walls were enlargements of snippets of film he'd obtained in this way. He'd blow up the various parts according to a fixed ratio and then make a clay model. Then, fitting the parts to the model in much the same process as a cobbler applying leather to a wooden form and stitching up a shoe, he sewed his rubber doll together. But in terms of difficulty, there was no comparison between the respective tasks. First of all, he had to take great pains to get hold of rubber that had the actual color and softness of your skin. Touching it, I was reminded of the waterproof cloth that's used for women's raincoats —a thin layer of rubber over a silk ground. It was very much like that, only closer to the feel of human skin. He tried ordering material from shops all around the country—Osaka, Kobe, Tokyo—and finally found some that pleased him at his fifth attempt. And when it came to stitching the bits of material together, not only did he fit them onto the clay form he had made, but, for those portions that he found particularly difficult or unsatisfactory, he actually applied them to living "models." He would take a sewn-up rubber pouch all the way to Shizuoka and try fitting it on the breasts of F...ko of the X House. He would go off to Nagano and have a fitting using the buttocks of S...ko of the O House. It was the same with the shoulders of K...ko in Tokyo's Asakusa, and the backbone of A...ko in Osaka, with a woman's knees from Hōjō in Chiba, and another's neck from the Beppu hot springs in Kyushu. He did fittings in all these places.

But how did he manage to create those flushed lips, those pearly teeth inside? How did he succeed in implanting that lustrous hair and those long eyelashes? How did he inset those vivacious eyes? How did he create that tongue, those nails? If asked what they were made of, he retreated behind a shroud of mystery, saying with a smile "That's my secret!"; but that shadowy smile hinted at horrifying things. One suspected they were the product of some unspeakable vice, something truly sordid, and it made one shudder. Those rubber dolls I'd heard about which sailors use for company on long voyages can't ever have been half as true to life. If it were just a matter of patching together rubber pouches into a more or less human shape, there would be nothing to wonder at, but *these* rubber dolls had proper nostrils, and in those nostrils, snot. They had exactly the same body temperature as human beings, and body odor. They had an oily feel to them. Saliva emerged from their lips and sweat from their armpits. And why had he gone to the trouble of making thirty of such dolls? It was because a variety of poses was required, such as the sitting-on-the-lap pose, the standing embrace, the ****** and ******.

"This is how it works!" he declared, and to my horror he proceeded to give a demonstration of the particular forms his pleasure took, with the dolls as partners (he'd kept his spirits up by continuous drinking), accompanying it all with various obscene remarks.

"How do you suppose this snot tastes?" he said, inviting me to try. "Oh yes, I remember now: you said only a fool would lick his wife's dribble up.... Well, look ... how I ... lick it up. And that's nothing! Now I'll—" And before I knew it, he was lying face up on the floor, with a doll squatting with its thighs spread right on top of his face. He reached both hands up and pressed hard against its abdomen. From the hole in the doll's buttocks came the sound of gas escaping. Sticky fecal matter began to flow over the old man's face and onto his bald skull. I didn't wait to see more, but leapt out of the nearest window and ran as fast as I could down the pitch-dark country road.

~ ‖ ~

My darling Yurako, these are the facts I've been wanting to reveal to you. I hope that you'll be able to just pass this account off with a laugh, that the curse will stop with me, that you'll go on leading a pleasant life. After all this, however, the idea of making movies with you has lost any appeal it had—indeed, it fills me with a sort of dread. I can't help feeling that my making you a star and shooting film after film centering on your gorgeous body has ended in you being stolen from me by that dirty old man. All unawares, you've been stripped naked by him, and your hands and feet and every part of you have been made to serve his pleasure. And if only it were just that! I used to think that my lovely, darling Yurako was like no one else on earth, that she belonged to me entirely; but ever since that night, that faith of mine has been shaken. Your body is scattered throughout the country! It's also lying folded up on a shelf in an old man's bedroom closet! You're just one of those many "Yurakos," per- haps just a shadow of yourself. When thoughts like this well up inside me, no matter how tightly I hold you, it doesn't feel like it's the real, one-of-a-kind "you." And, just as you may have become a shadow, I've come to seem like one as well.

The love we had, though not utterly destroyed by this, has been turned into something hollow and deceptive, and more impermanent than a single film shot. It's too late for regrets, of course; and yet, if only I hadn't met the old man that night. . . . I've often prayed that everything that happened then might be a dream; that the old man himself and the eerie house on top of the hill might be an illusion which would vanish without a trace. But I've gone past that hill many times since then, by night and by day, and the house is actu- ally there—there's no denying it.

By now I have a good idea as to who the old man is, his name and social position. And not only that—I've met A. . .ko of the B House in Osaka, the one who has your backbone; and F. . .ko from

Shizuoka, who has your breasts; and the women with your shoulders, your buttocks, your neck. I've determined that the old man was by no means lying. It seems the women never learned his real name, but they all said that he was a sexual pervert of a rare sort; that he often brought along camera equipment and rubber pouches, and made outrageous demands; and that he always addressed them as "Yurako."

But Yurako, my one and only, real Yurako! I don't want to tell you that man's name and position. And please, don't try to find out for yourself. This is the one thing I'm going to keep from you now, as I face the end. Comforted by the thought that I'll be able to meet the real you in the *next* life, I can now take leave of this present one, this world of illusion in which we live.

$\mathcal{M}$anganese Dioxide Dreams

TRANSLATED BY
Anthony H. Chambers

August 8, morning

To Tokyo on the Ideyu Express. There are four of us: my wife and I, Tamako, and the maid Fuji. Throughout July the heat was the worst in recent memory, but late at night on the fourth of this month we finally saw some rain, and the temperature fell nine degrees to endurable levels. We thought the worst was over, but this morning the high temperatures returned. Having bought the Ideyu tickets last night, we braved the intense heat and set out. At 10:27 we got off at Shimbashi Station, then came directly to the Hasegawa inn at Toranomon and had a rest. For the last several years I've tried to avoid Tokyo at the height of summer, but this year my blood pressure has gradually improved. I came once last month; this is my second visit. In the old days one expected Tokyo to be cooler in the summer than Osaka and Kyoto, but this is no longer the case. As we headed from Shimbashi toward Toranomon along the street where the trolley runs, our automobile stopped again and again, and with each stop the heat inside rose to unbearable levels. After a short rest at the inn, my wife, Tamako, and Fuji went out to shop and have lunch at Ketel's in Ginza, promising to return at 1:30. I watched the second half of *Blue Continent* at the Marunouchi Nikkatsu, then came back to the inn, had a piece of toast and a bottle of orange juice, and settled in for my daily nap. As if the sweltering heat weren't enough, though, the inn is being enlarged, and the construction noise is terrible. A building of many stories is going up across the street, too. The constant din of concrete being poured and of iron rods being hammered is deafening. Automobiles and motorcycles, too, produce a lot of noise and vibration as they pass the inn; traffic is probably heavy here because the Mutual Aid Hall and the former Manchurian Railroad Building are nearby. Reluctantly I take a little of the sleeping drug I brought along just in case but haven't used in a long time, and doze for thirty or forty minutes.

Our main purpose in coming to Tokyo this time is to visit the KR Company warehouse in Kyōbashi tomorrow morning to sort out Etsuko's wedding robes and chests, which had been stored separately in our Kyoto and Atami houses and at a relative's place in Tokyo and then were put together in the warehouse with some of her other household furniture and effects. We've nothing in particular to do today. For some time my wife and Tamako have been saying they want me to take them to a strip show. Apparently they've decided to force me to accompany them this afternoon to the Nichigeki Music Hall. They began putting pressure me on last year to take them, saying it was awkward for women to go alone. Then, if my guess is correct, they developed a sudden desire to attend a live performance after seeing a burlesque film called "Naked Goddesses" (original title, *Ah! Les Belles Bacchantes!*)—a hit in Paris—at the Kyōgeki on Kawaramachi this spring. I told them that the few women who patronize such places are good-time girls keeping foreigners company, and that I'd never seen a respectable married or single woman there; it'd be best if they gave up the idea, but, if they were so determined to go, they should go with someone else. It would be in poor taste, I thought, for the head of a household to escort his wife and her younger sister there. Until today, then, I've excused myself from accompanying my family, though I have gone by myself. But last month Mitsuko (Tamako's daughter-in-law), who lives in Kitashirakawa, couldn't endure any more of the Kyoto heat and escaped with

Miori to Izu Heights. Leaving Miori with Tamako one day, she went to Tokyo and bravely entered the Music Hall, where she saw "There Are Seven Keys to Love," which included in its credits such names as Tōgō Seiji, Muramatsu Shōfū, and Mishima Yukio. When she came back, she said that it may be called a strip show, but there was nothing so improper about it, the dancers were adorable, the audience included a number of women, and the girl called Gypsy Rose was especially pretty. "It wouldn't be odd at all for you to go to a show like that," she told her aunt and mother-in-law. With this prompting, they turned to me: "There, you see? Now will you take us?"—which explains how our present undertaking came about.

As they promised, my wife and the others came back to the inn after one o'clock. The four of us set out immediately. Arriving in front of the Nichigeki, we disposed of Fuji by sending her off to see a movie of her choice. The three of us then bought tickets for the back row of reserved seating in the Music Hall, where we'd be as inconspicuous as possible. The program, having changed since Mitsuko went, featured "The Pleasures of Temptation" in twenty scenes, produced and written by Maruo Chōken, including "Aqua Girl's Bottom-up Mambo." About fifteen minutes after we entered the theater, the show began. At most, sixty or seventy percent of the seats in front of us were occupied, all by foreigners. The other Japanese people sat in the unreserved section, which was seventy or eighty percent full. A few more customers trickled in after the show had started. A man and woman, apparently Americans, entered the reserved section and sat in our row. Then two or three GIs, with girlfriends in tow, lined up in the row ahead of us. Aside from the American lady and the GIs' girls, my wife and Tamako appeared to be the only women in the hall. No doubt it was a rare event here to see not just one but two kimono-clad ladies beyond middle age. To reach this theater, you have to take the elevator to the top of the Nichigeki and then climb a flight of stairs. With its low ceiling, the place is as stuffy and cramped as an attic. The OSK Music Hall in Osaka is more comfortable. Our establishment was air-conditioned, but only enough to make us feel a momentary chill when we entered; once we took our seats, it got muggy, and we waved our fans continuously. From the opening scene—the mambo contest—to the grand finale nineteen scenes later, the program consumed a full two hours. The many luscious nude figures linger in my memory only as a jumbled kaleidoscope—I have no idea which girl played what role in which episode. This sort of thing is probably best seen once and then forgotten completely. Halfway through, my wife began to doze off. " 'Naked Goddesses' was better," she grumbled. "These can't compare with French nudes." She added, "The dancing girls are pretty, but I didn't expect to see so many men on stage." I agreed with her in this—the production included far too many male roles for my taste. Gypsy Rose, whom Mitsuko had praised to the skies, seems to be the prima donna here, but she's past her prime and has too much fat on her, and there's a Eurasian cast to her features. All in all, she's not my type, and my wife and Tamako say they feel the same way. I found a girl called Harukawa Masumi far more attractive. (I didn't mention *this* to my wife.) I've forgotten all the other scenes except number sixteen, "The Back Window." An old man, after checking into his hotel room, happens to look at the window across the way and is thrilled to see a nubile beauty in the bath, displaying her torso, bottom, back, legs, and feet, from the tips to the soles, as she washes herself. Then a bald man, apparently her husband, joins her in the bath, where a certain amount of sweet-talk ensues. Utterly deflated, the hotel guest collapses in a heap. The bathing beauty in this skit is Harukawa Masumi. Even in Japan, such well-developed breasts, buttocks, and legs are not uncommon these days, but generally I feel no particular attraction unless they're accompanied by a feline sort of face, the kind that Simone Simon used to have.

In the evening, back to the Hasegawa for a short rest. We went for dinner to a Chinese restaurant in Tamurachō. Because I tend to over-eat, I gave up Chinese food for a long while, after developing high blood pressure, and had it again for the first time only last month, at the Tōtōtei. This, then, was my second time. We had a platter of *hors d'oeuvres*, including jellyfish steeped in sesame oil and soy sauce, *shiitake* mushrooms, white chicken meat, abalone, tomatoes, and cucumbers; shrimp wrapped in paper and deep-fried; a soup called "lotus and fish-wings," made of shark's fins and egg whites; walnuts and seared chicken simmered in soy; braised tofu and chick-en; almond soup and "eight-treasures" rice with date jam; and, fi-nally, tea on boiled rice with sharp Chinese pickles. I used to love these pickles, but I don't touch them now as they're bad for hyper-tension. According to Fuji, whose father works in a Kyushu coal mine, similar pickles are eaten around Fukuoka. They make her home-sick, she said, wolfing them down. After dinner I went straight back to the Hasegawa, while my wife and Tamako took a turn around the Ginza. We sent Fuji to the relative's place in Akasaka.

On the morning of the ninth we waited for Fuji to come to the Hasegawa at about nine o'clock, whereupon the three women set off to sort out the items in the warehouse. Staying at the inn for the morning, I asked several publishers to come and discuss some busi-ness. When we'd finished, a little before noon, I went to the Hibiya Motion Picture Theater to see the controversial film *Les Diaboliques*. Atami has movie theaters too, four of them, but they rarely show for-eign films that don't appeal to a general audience, nor are they air-conditioned or heated, which makes them unbearable for an elderly person in midsummer and midwinter. I wait for opportunities to come to Tokyo—indeed, in my case the main reason for coming to Tokyo is usually to see plays and films. *Les Diaboliques* was written and directed by Henri-Georges Clouzot, who specializes in thrillers and previously made *The Wages of Fear*. One doesn't know until the last moment who the villain is, and the film is preceded by a courteous message asking viewers not to discuss the plot, so as not to spoil the enjoyment of those who have yet to see it. The tale revolves around three people: Michel, headmaster of a private elementary school called the Institut Delasalle, in a suburb of Paris; his wife, Christina, who owns the school and teaches there; and Nicole, another teacher there, who is the headmaster's mistress. Michel, the headmaster, is played by Paul Meurisse; Christina by Véra Clouzot, the director's wife; and Nicole, the mistress-teacher, by Simone Signoret. Christina is a wealthy South American who has invested in the school; suffering from heart disease and timid by nature, she does whatever her cruel, despotic husband, Michel, demands. In addition, as she and every other instructor and pupil in the school are aware, she has lost her husband to her colleague Nicole. Although Michel appears to prefer his mistress to his wife, he doesn't treat her with much affection: his abuse of her is little different from the way he treats his wife. Just when Christina, the wife, can no longer bear her husband's brutality, Nicole, the mistress, proposes that the two of them kill him. Christina is shocked at the idea, but is finally persuaded.

Nicole invites Christina on a three-day holiday, loading a wicker trunk just large enough to hold a person into the school's baggage truck before going to stay at her house in a rural village called Niort. From there she has Christina telephone Michel and ask for a divorce. Since Michel has no intention of divorcing his financial backer, he comes rushing to the house to dissuade her. Nicole, saying this is an opportunity they can't miss, mixes a few drops of a powerful sleeping drug into some whiskey, hands it to Christina, and, when Christina hesitates, urges her angrily to give it to her husband to drink. Carrying the drugged Michel to the bathroom, the two women dump him in the tub, and Nicole holds his head underwater to drown him. They then stuff his body in the wicker trunk, place it in the truck, and drive through the night back to the school, where they heave him into the swimming pool. No one is the wiser and everything has gone according to plan: drunk, Michel has fallen into the pool, and his body will soon rise to the surface—but by dawn, it still hasn't appeared. A series of mysterious events follows.

Christina deliberately drops her room key into the pool and has a pupil search for it. The pupil emerges from the water with a key, but the key is not Christina's, it's the one to Michel's room. Christina instructs the janitor to drain the pool, but the body has disappeared without a trace. Several days later, a familiar suit is delivered from the cleaners: it's the one Michel wore that night. The faculty and pupils gather in front of the schoolhouse for a commemorative photograph, which, when developed, shows the headmaster's face reflected dimly in a window. One of the pupils says that he has been punished by the headmaster for breaking a window. Late at night, footsteps that sound like Michel's can be heard, and the pecking of a typewriter comes from the headmaster's office. Tormented by fear day and night, Christina, who has a bad heart, becomes a semi-invalid. Finally, one night she discovers Michel—is it his ghost?— submerged in the bath-tub, just as he was that night. The moment Michel rises from the tub, water streaming from his body, Christina cries out, falls back against the door, and, her eyes turning up in their sockets, expires. Nicole, who has been away, suddenly reappears. Michel hugs and kisses her. "Even with heart disease, she was a tough one. She put us to a lot of trouble," he says. At this point a private detective, who has been sus-picious all along, enters and arrests the pair, saying as he leads them away, "You'll get out after you've served fifteen or twenty years."

Thus the plot takes a sudden turn when Christina dies and Michel embraces Nicole, and, until a few minutes before this, the viewer is gripped with suspense over the outcome. In retrospect, though, one sees that this film concentrates too much on thrilling the viewer and contains too many implausibilities. In particular, it's absurd for the headmaster and his mistress to believe they won't be found out, even as they employ such complicated, laborious methods to murder his wife. It would make for better theater to have the crime go undetected. It's also absurd for the pair immediately to be exposed and arrested. The process by which the detective sniffs out their vicious plan is unclear. In his attempt to shock his heart-patient wife to death, the headmaster plays dead in the tub, is tossed around for hours in a trunk, and is dumped into a pool. That's fine, if the outcome is successful (as it is here), but things might have gone wrong: the conspiracy might come to light before she dies of shock; the shock might be insufficient to cause her death. Would he and his mistress become so absorbed in their troublesome project without considering such risks as these? It's also unclear where Michel hides, from the time he's thrown into the pool until he reappears before his wife as a ghost. In short, this is a film that simply frightens its audience for a time; once the scary gimmicks are understood, it appears as nothing but an empty sham. Nevertheless, it's the fine acting, and the ingenious processes by which the audience is strung along, that account for the popularity and high praise the picture has won for itself. One magazine called it "a thriller with a perfect score for terror," "a truly creepy film," "a film so frightening that timid women won't want to go home alone at night." Viewing a trailer of the film last month, when I went to see *Nana*, I was drawn to Simone Signoret's extraordinarily cruel look as she plays Nicole. The Japanese translation of the film title—*Akuma no yō na onna* ("a diabolical woman")—suits that look well. A large, faintly unclean face; dull, weary skin; a woman who looks unfeeling, unafraid, and devious—without this type of woman cast in the central role, the picture could never be as spine-chilling as it aims to be. Here is a woman, one feels, capable of grasping her lover's head with both hands and pushing it underwater. Véra Clouzot, too, is well suited to the role of Christina, looking the part of a sickly wife oppressed by her husband and his mistress. The highlight of her performance is in her movements and expression at the instant she suffers a heart attack and collapses. This was the first time I'd seen a Western woman die in this way, even in a motion picture. Losing consciousness, she gradually slides down against the closed door behind her and slumps over to one side. This posture affords the audience the best possible view of her face in her last moments, and the sight is as memorable as the corpse of a huge insect whose life has abruptly been cut short. Her eyes, in contrast to Nicole's venomous, glittering orbs, are the frightened, narrow, weak eyes of a constantly tyrannized woman; but suddenly they open wide to reveal the whites, the pupils roll to the upper right, and all movement ceases. Michel steps calmly from the tub, as if to say, "That did the trick," comes to her side, gazes at her face, grasps her arm and then releases it with a looks that says, "Finally!" The scenes that arouse the greatest sense of horror are those in which Nicole pushes Michel underwater in the tub, Christina dies from shock, and Michel, having risen from the tub, removes the false eyes he has inserted to frighten his wife. These eyes are thin, convex lenses designed to fit snugly against the real corneas. Michel, playing dead, wears them to make his death-face look all the more ghastly. Even I was startled when he stuck both hands into his eyes and pulled out those lenses; the woman sitting next to me gasped and covered her face.

I left the theater at about two o'clock. On the street, the temperature was as high as yesterday's. Because of the heat, I'd had a soft ice cream inside the theater; now I felt extremely thirsty again. Going to the basement level of the Sanshin Building, across the street, I had another ice cream and two slices of cake, then hailed a taxi and returned to the Hasegawa. There I found that my wife and the other two women had wrapped up their business at the warehouse early and gone to the Hibiya Motion Picture Theater, where, until shortly before, they'd been watching the same film as I had; but, afraid they might keep me waiting beyond our appointed time, they'd left the theater in the middle of the film and had come back here forty or fifty minutes ago, they said. They were, then, in the theater at the same time I was. Since my wife herself has been told by the doctor that her heart is weak and has always been scared of getting a shock of some kind, she'd been in two minds about this film, both wanting to see it and afraid to; but in time she learned the story from people who'd seen it already, and she began to say, "It doesn't bother me any more, I want to see it, too." Nevertheless, considering that she left halfway through, I suppose she was still nervous about her heart. When I told her that the second half was more frightening than the first, and that Christina's death and Michel's removing his false eyes were genuinely hair-raising, she said, "In that case, I'm glad I didn't stay."

After that, we rested for an hour or two. Checking out of the Hasegawa at five o'clock, we stopped by the Komatsu Store and some other shops in the Ginza, then, arriving at the Yaesu side of Tokyo Station, ate dinner at Tsujitome, in the basement of Daimaru. The Kyoto cuisine at Tsujitome is one of the delights that draws us from Atami into Tokyo. In recent years, especially, having business in the Tokyo area and unsure when we might be able to go back to Kyoto, we've keenly looked forward to it. What we most covet at this time of year are *ayu* trout and *hamo* eel. In the summer at Atami there's plenty of bonito and tuna, but the *ayu* come from the Hayakawa and Kanogawa rivers and can't compare with the *ayu* from the Hozu Gorge. *Hamo*, too, can sometimes be had in the Izu

Heights region now, and we occasionally try it, but the taste is inferior and the bones aren't cut properly, so that we end up longing for Kansai *hamo* all the more. Recently my wife, who doesn't eat bonito because it smells fishy, has been saying she wanted to go to Tokyo soon for the "peony" *hamo* at Tsujitome. Peony *hamo*, consisting of eel boiled in arrowroot starch and served with *shiitake* and greens in the soup bowls Tsujitome is noted for, is rather thick and mellow for a Japanese clear soup. Tonight's menu at Tsujitome was: slices of raw, young sea bass, rinsed in cold water; red-miso soup with loach and burdock root sliced as thin as bamboo leaves; a small dish of eggplant and black-eyed peas dressed in sesame, and sardines simmered with ginger and pickled plum; a small dish of fried young taro, with simmered chicken and yellow wheat-gluten dumplings; a small dish of fine, cold noodles; a small dish of rice pressed from a round mold, garnished with Nara pickles and ginger; *hamo* broiled with soy, and the long-awaited peony *hamo*; and, on top of all that, large *ayu*, which they said they'd ordered from Kyoto, grilled with salt and served with knotweed vinegar—an unexpected treat. Finally, we were offered arrowroot cakes from the Tsuruya Hachiman, in Osaka, but we were too full to touch them. With Japanese food, I don't normally worry about overeating, but after all this I felt as though I'd consumed more calories than I would have with Western or Chinese food, and worried that my blood pressure might have risen. After dinner we hurried straight to the station platform and boarded an 8:21 train which, apparently because of an accident of some kind, was delayed for a few minutes. At that hour the second-class coaches shouldn't be crowded, but tonight they were full as far as Ofuna, the ripe smell of humanity making the damp heat all the worse. We arrived at Atami just before eleven o'clock. As soon as we reached the house, I bathed, changed into a light summer kimono, stepped onto the garden grass and, reclining in a deck chair, gazed at the night view of the Izu Peninsula. A waning moon hung in the sky; Izu Heights, Atami, Ajiro, and Kawana were dotted with lights. Recalling the heat of Tokyo yesterday and today, I felt as though this hilltop cottage were in another world.

After we went to sleep, I was woken by the sound of my wife moaning at around two or three o'clock and quickly tried to wake her up. With several strong shakes I finally succeeded. Recently she's been complaining of nightmares and shortness of breath during the night, and she often lets out sudden, alarming groans. One possible cause is her bedsprings, which, by sagging under the torso, might be putting pressure on her heart. Though I use a bed of the same design, I don't experience this problem, so it must be the particular defect in her heart that accounts for the difference. In any case, we intend soon to have someone from the furniture store adjust the springs. Because a small night table stands between our beds, my hands can't reach her immediately, even when I'm in a hurry to awaken her; I have to get out of my bed and step over to hers. In the excitement, I sometimes wake up completely and find myself unable to go back to sleep. My wife says she's gripped by an indescribable sensation when she has a nightmare: she can hardly breathe for two or three minutes, however much she tries, and she feels as though she might die on the spot. It's not uncommon, then, for her to stay awake after one of these episodes, propping herself up and reading until dawn. Even without the problem of the springs, the strain on her heart must have been excessive tonight, after we'd feasted two evenings in a row on Chinese cuisine and the delicacies at Tsujitome. I, too, had trouble falling asleep after being roused by those groans, and tossed about uncomfortably. Normally a sound sleeper, I'm able to doze off again quickly when I've had to use the toilet during the night; but tonight my stomach felt extremely full from overindulging like that. Then I suddenly realized that my pulse was skipping a beat, something that hasn't occurred for some time. The pauses came at regular intervals, after every three beats, and an artery would twitch each time. Though no pain accompanies this event, the feeling is not a pleasant one, as the clear implication is that something is wrong with my heart. I always feel the twitching in an artery—now in the upper chest, near the shoulder; now farther down, on the side; now on the right side of the left breast, or on the left side of the right breast; but tonight I felt it in the solar plexus, right above my stomach. I've been warned by the doctor that overeating is likely to bring on an irregular pulse. It goes without saying that the sensation in my solar plexus was retribution for two days of *ayu*, peony *hamo*, "eight-treasures" rice, and "lotus with fish-wings." Knowing that it's best at such times to use sleeping pills to blur the consciousness and relieve the anxiety, I swallowed one tablet of Rabona and two of Adalin, and gradually slipped into a state of half-wakefulness, half-sleep. It's a quirk of mine to enjoy a fuzzy state like this, in which I'm not quite sure whether I'm asleep or awake. Half-conscious at first, I enjoy the myriad vague imaginings, now forming, now vanishing, like foam on the sea, until at some point they merge with real dreams. *Now they'll turn into dreams,* I say in my semi-conscious state, as I watch them unfold. What explanation Freud offers in *The Interpretation of Dreams*, or how it is with other people, I don't know, but I feel as though I'm able, to some extent, to sense in advance what my dreams will be and even at times to control them. There will be those who say that the whole thing is a dream, that when I wake up I'll realize that I've been dreaming within a dream; but I can't necessarily agree. . . . As I turn this way and that, conscious of the pressure in my overfull stomach and wishing that the sleeping pills would quickly take effect, I think of last night's peony *hamo*: the pure white flesh of the eel, the limpid, slippery semi-liquid that encased it. It feels as if it's thrashing about in my stomach, unchanged in form. From the white flesh floats an image of Harukawa Masumi in the bathtub, washing the various parts of her body. Arrowroot-starch dressing . . . that slimy sauce coating not *hamo* but her—Harukawa Masumi . . . wait, now it's Michel, the headmaster of the Institut Delasalle, in the tub. Simone Signoret, his mistress, is pushing him under. Michel is dead. Wet hair clings to his forehead and covers his eyes; through gaps in the hair I can see the dead man's huge eyeballs, turned up in their sockets.

Then another weird figment makes its entrance. In my library I have my own, private, Western-style toilet, on which I think up marvelous things as I do my business every morning. This toilet came to mind. Installing a Western-style fixture has to do with the views of Dr. Fusé, of the Osaka National Hospital: he advises anyone with high blood pressure to avoid Japanese toilets, because when an old person bears down in a squatting position he's likely to suffer a cerebral hemorrhage. On this basis I've installed a toilet with a seat; but it has the added advantage of being most convenient for inspecting one's own excrement. A Japanese flush-style fixture displays its contents so openly that one can't bear to look; in the Western design, however, the feces are submerged in water, so that one can observe them at one's leisure, as though viewing something that's been surgically removed and preserved in alcohol. One can detect a bloody stool, for example—the result of a stomach ulcer or uterine cancer—at an early stage. Recently I noticed that the water turned bright red whenever I had a bowel movement, and I passed several anxious days suspecting an ulcer, until I was relieved to learn that the source was the red beets I enjoy eating at breakfast. I assume that bloody stool from a stomach ulcer has a blackish tone, but in the case of red beets, beautiful crimson threads ooze from the excrement and tint the surrounding water, so that it looks like pale manganese-dioxide water. The color is so lovely I sometimes gaze at it for some time, captivated. The feces floating in this crimson solution are not at all repulsive. At times a fecal lump will suggest the shape of something else, such as a human face. Tonight one looks like Simone Signoret's diabolical face, glaring at me from the red liquid. I study it, reluctant to flush the water away.... Like fluid clay, it contorts and twists and congeals again, now into the form of a sculpted, Grecian torso. "The Basic Annals of Empress Lü," in *Records of the Grand Historian*,[1] says: "Finally, the empress dowager cut off Lady Ch'i's arms and legs, gouged out her eyes, deafened her ears with poisonous smoke, gave her a potion to drink which made her mute, and had her placed in a latrine pit, calling her a 'human sow.'" Simone Signoret's face has turned into a human sow, I see....

I wonder how the human sow came to mind. The passage "Though she might not meet as sad an end as Lady Ch'i" appears in the main text of "The Sacred Tree," on page 150 of my revised translation of *The Tale of Genji*, and the note says: "Wife of the Han emperor Kao Tsu. After Kao Tsu's death, she incurred the jealousy of Empress Lü, who cut off her arms and legs, plucked out her eyes, and placed her in a privy." Did my desire one day to write something based on this account chance to merge with the image in the flush toilet?

> *Empress Dowager Lü was Kao Tsu's consort when he was a commoner. She bore him Emperor Hui the Filial and the queen mother, Princess Yuan of Lu. When Kao Tsu became king of Han he acquired Lady Ch'i of Tingt'ao and loved her dearly. She bore him Ju Yi, the Melancholy King of Chao. Hui the Filial was kindhearted and weak. Kao Tsu thought him different from himself.... The beloved Lady Ch'i always accompanied the emperor when he*

---

[1] The *Shih Chi of Ssu-ma Ch'ien* (ca. 145–86 B.C.), which has been translated by Burton Watson as *Records of the Grand Historian* (London and New York: Columbia University Press, 1961). The section on Empress Lü can be found in vol. 1, pp. 321–23.

went east of the Pass, and day and night wept and wailed, begging that her own son be set up in place of the heir apparent. Empress Lü, being advanced in years, always stayed behind, rarely saw the emperor, and was more and more neglected.... In the Fourth Month, the day chia-ch'en in the twelfth year of his reign, Kao Tsu died in the Palace of Lasting Joy.... Empress Lü nurtured the greatest hatred for Lady Ch'i and her son, the king of Chao. She immediately had Lady Ch'i confined to her apartments and summoned the king of Chao.... Emperor Hui the Filial, compassionate and aware of the empress dowager's anger, went himself to meet the king of Chao at the Pa River, accompanied him to the palace, and protected him, eating and sleeping with him. The empress dowager wanted to kill the king of Chao, but could find no opportunity. In the Twelfth Month of the first year of Hui the Filial's reign, the emperor went out at dawn to hunt pheasants. The king of Chao, being young, could not get up so early. The empress dowager heard that he was alone and sent someone with poison to give him to drink. When Emperor Hui the Filial returned, the king of Chao was already dead.... Finally, the empress dowager cut off Lady Ch'i's arms and legs ... calling her a "human sow." After a few days, she summoned Emperor Hui the Filial and showed him the "human sow." Hui the Filial looked at her and asked who it was, and only then did he realize that it was Lady Ch'i. He wept bitterly, fell ill as a result, and for more than a year was unable to rise from his bed. He sent someone to the empress dowager to say, "This was not the act of a human being. I, as your son, can never govern the empire." From then on, Hui the Filial indulged every day in drink and dissipation and paid no heed to governance.

This is what *Records of the Grand Historian* has to say. A note in the

Compilation of Han Writings in Japanese Translation explains that the character *chih* means "sow" or "mother hog," and "human sow" refers to a person who has become like an "old female pig." The *Compilation* clarifies other unusual terms, as well.

There, floating in the beautiful, crimson, manganese-dioxide water, is an object resembling a limbless torso or a lump of pork. As I'm examining it, someone says, "Look, that's a human sow in there." I turn to see a woman standing at my side, dressed in the robes of a Han empress dowager. "Oh, no!—the 'human sow' must be Lady Ch'i," I exclaim, quickly covering my eyes. I realize that the aristocratic lady beside me is Empress Dowager Lü, and I am Emperor Hui the Filial. . . . Suddenly I'm awake. It's 4:30 A.M., and a pale light glows beyond the *shōji*. I hear the drum of the Kōa Kannon Temple, on top of the hill. My stomach is still uncomfortably distended. At some point my wife has fallen into a peaceful sleep. Where did the real dream begin? When Simone Signoret's face started to twist and crumble? . . . And thinking these thoughts, I drift off to sleep again.

（英文版）谷崎潤一郎短編集
THE GOURMET CLUB

2001 年 5 月25日　　第 1 刷発行

著　者　谷崎 潤一郎
訳　者　アンソニー・チェンバーズ
　　　　ポール・マッカーシー
発行者　野間佐和子
発行所　講談社インターナショナル株式会社
　　　　〒112-8652 東京都文京区音羽 1-17-14
　　　　電話　03-3944-6493（編集部）
　　　　　　　03-3944-6492（営業部・業務部）
　　　　ホームページ　http://www.kodansha-intl.co.jp
印刷所　株式会社 平河工業社
製本所　黒柳製本株式会社

落丁本・乱丁本は、小社業務部宛にお送りください。送料小社負担にてお取替えします。なお、この本についてのお問い合わせは、編集部宛にお願いいたします。本書の無断複写（コピー）、転載は著作権法の例外を除き、禁じられています。

定価はカバーに表示してあります。

© Kanze Emiko
English translation © Kodansha International 2001
Printed in Japan
ISBN 4-7700-2690-0